An Unseemly Love

A Novel

Kim Benton

Copyright © 2023 by Kim Benton

All rights reserved. This book or any portion thereof may not be reproduced or used in any manner whatsoever without the express written permission of the publisher except for the use of brief quotations in a book review.

ISBN: 978-1-304-90714-1

Produced by iWriteBooks Publishing, Atlanta, GA
iWriteBooksPub.com
MyuniqueGreen.com

For my husband and our three children, thank you for making my life positively full.

For my husband and our three children, thank you for making my life beautifully full.

Chapter One

Meeka

For August, it's really a pleasant night. Not too hot and there's a nice breeze in the air. You can feel the excitement of the fall semester starting up and a resolve in everyone to make it a great year. My new school year resolution is to be more social. All my friends tell me I'm a prude and act like I'm fifty instead of twenty. So here I am. I'm not sure what I was really thinking. Nikki always has a way of getting me to do things that my better judgment goes totally against. College Saturday night football at the hottest sports bar in town was not the place to be if you really want to be alone. It's not that I don't enjoy being out on the town with my girl, using our fake ID's to sip on wine, but I hate to be pressed by guys that I know at the end of the night are not my type.

I'm not interested in wasting anyone's time, especially not mine—I also can't stand being in crowded places where perverts take the opportunity to rub up against you.

But here we are, it's wall-to-wall and nowhere to sit.

The men are all over the place and I know this is exactly where Nikki wants to be. It's the start of the college football season and two major rivals are playing tonight. I really like football; it's just I prefer to be at the game live. Hanging out at a bar watching big screens just does not do much for me. If I don't have bored written all over my face, my body language is sending signals that I hope will run the guys away. I don't want to leave my girl hanging, but I really don't plan to be standing around all night long.

Nikki and I have been best friends since our freshman year in college. She is the type of friend that everybody needs at least one of. Since we were assigned to the same dorm room, we hit it off day one. We have this perfect complimentary thing going on. She's outgoing in a wild and crazy kind of way and I'm more conservative. She does things in a more spontaneous manner and I'm more calculated in my adventures.

Don't get me wrong; being majorettes, we have some things in common. I'm not trying to be braggadocios, but we are both cute. Nikki is what some would call a firecracker. She has me by fifteen pounds equally divided between her breasts, hips, and butt. She has a milky way complexion with a short crop hairstyle to die for if you like short hair.

Her legs are every guy's dream.

They're long enough to fit her 5'9 frame, but short enough not to make her taller than the average male. Everything she wears is skintight, back out and much cleavage. She's not a freak, but if there was such a term as border line ho; then that's my girl. If the dictionary had pictures by the words, Nik's picture would be by the word "real". She plays hard and she loves even harder. This is our fourth year together as friends and I can't recall needing her and her not being there. When I made lead majorette our freshman year, which is unheard of, I think every other majorette on the squad hated me. Nikki was the only one that gave me my props and gave me the respect that I deserved.

Okay, we've circled the place twice now and no one is giving up or offering up seats. I've spilled more wine than I have drunk trying my best not to let one of these fools touch me. I really don't think I'm better than anyone, but I get a lot of flak from the females on campus. I'm not after anybody's man and I don't do a lot of flirting. I can't help that their men just don't seem to understand what faithful means. Nikki is always fussing at me about caring what other people think or feel. I just would prefer to be liked than to be seen as a threat to other women.

On my last scan of the place before I tell Nikki goodnight, I see my mother's, best friend's husband. I have to give it to Michael—he gets out. This must be my lucky night as he and two of his boys are sitting at a corner booth for five or six people. I really have never understood why Diane puts up with him. From the late-night calls to my mother, she is constantly crying over him. If he has not been cheating on her, then he is out gambling into the morning hours.

He's what I would call a professional with thug tendencies.

He is an engineer at a car manufacturing company making good money, but something about the drinking, gambling and ho hounding I guess is in his genes. Anyway, he has always been nice to me and nothing but respectful, so hopefully he is in a sharing mood, meaning his table. I get Nikki's attention and tell her to follow me towards Michael's table. I do have to give it to Michael he knows how to enjoy himself. They've got appetizers, Heineken, and his favorite cognac in abundance. Although my mother acts like she does not care for him, whenever he is around everyone has a good time. He has this charisma and charm about him that is warm and inviting. I guess that's why the women can't stay away.

Michael and Diane have been married for four years. Since Diane and my mom have been best friends for over twenty years, Michael is like family. Diane is ten years his senior and my mom did everything she could to get Diane not to marry Michael, but she was passed being in love with him. Since Diane was thirty-six when they got married and already had a sixteen-year-old daughter, Michael's confession that he did not want to have a child was Diane's sign that they were meant to be together. Although at forty now, Diane is very attractive and in shape, I'm not sure that she will ever be enough for Michael. He just seems like his hunger can't be satisfied. I really hope that he settles down sooner versus later, because Diane is a sweet person and deserves to have a man that is as committed to her as she is to him.

I remember once my mom [mother crossed out] and dad had a small set at our house. It was probably about five couples and three or four single people. Michael was a little high and it was obvious that one of the single women was really flirting and coming on to him. The bad thing about it was that Michael was not sending any signals to discourage her. If anything, it was obvious that he would be a willing participant in whatever she wanted to do. The woman was dancing all up on Michael and caressing his face with her hands. My mother was furious and pulled Diane to the side to tell her she should straighten Michael out. As I was leaving the house, I saw Diane and Michael outside arguing. I don't know what happened, but they are still together.

Nikki is going into ho mode.

David is being a gentleman and letting her slide into the side of the table that he is occupying. Why her ass has to rub up against him, only she knows? David is Michael's best friend and an attorney. He is a handsome guy, but fine is not the best word to describe him, more so than distinguished. He is charming and very intelligent. If memory serves me correctly, he has a girlfriend. I should have told Nikki that we just wanted a seat and not to try and go home with the guys. The last thing I need is Michael going back to my dad and telling him his daughter was at a sports bar acting anything other than like the perfect little lady he raised me to be. It's bad enough I'm drinking wine and Michael knows I'm only twenty.

As Michael lets me slide into the side of the table he is on, he sweetly gives me the "what's up baby girl" greeting. I smile and tell him he's a life saver for me and my feet.

Hmmm......

I've never really noticed how handsome Michael Johnson is and he smells good. I'm not blind or anything but checking out my godmother's husband is not something I've done. However, tonight I'm really noticing how good looking he is.

Michael stands about 6'1. He's lean, but not skinny. I'm not hung up on complexion, so it's hard to describe—but if I had to say, he's like a shade of brown on cornbread that is perfectly. His hazel eyes are gentle, and at the same time, very dangerous. I love a man with a fresh haircut, and I swear I've never seen Michael not looking like he just stepped out of the barber shop. His hair is cut close and the natural waves he has lie smoothly against his perfectly shaped head. He has thin lips and beautiful teeth. Although Michael is thirty, he has a look that fits in anywhere. He has a nice green polo on that compliments his eyes and some faded designer jeans. I don't think I've ever met Michael's third friend, but he seems nice enough.

I'm feeling comfortable, and Michael and I are chatting casually. He has a great sense of humor and is being quite attentive. It's easy to talk with him and it seems we connect virtually on every point of our discussion. I've probably been around him a hundred times over the past four years, but I don't think we've ever had a meaningful conversation like tonight. It's usually about a football game or cracking jokes about my mom. Tonight, I'm noticing that he's not as superficial as I thought. He has this ability to engage you that's both intriguing and kind of scary. I mean good looking is one thing, but captivating is another.

I'm not sure if this is intentional, but Michael rarely calls me by my name, Meeka. Everything is always "baby girl" or "sweetheart". I think it's cute, but it makes me feel a little warm between my legs. Is it my imagination or does it feel like we are the only two people in this crowded sports bar? I know this place holds about two hundred people and there's every bit of three hundred people in here. The bar area with its modern look and feel and tables and booths are to capacity. I don't have a clue what Nikki, David or what's his name are talking about. I'm so tuned into Michael and entranced by his gaze. I find myself telling him why my ex and I split and how I am looking for more of a connection with a man before I take that leap into bed.

My ex, Jay, had me fooled for about nine months. He said he valued and respected my decision to maintain my virginity until I was completely sure that I was ready. I am not necessarily waiting on marriage, but I am waiting until I feel that the man I decide to give myself to is someone I could marry. I was Jay's trophy girlfriend. Lead majorette and football quarterback—the perfect couple on campus.

However, although Jay was waiting on me, he was not really waiting. He was screwing every cheerleader, sorority wannabe and new campus meat he could find. It was not hard to kick him to the curve, but it was hard to believe I had been so gullible. Evidence that a 4.0 GPA does not mean that you have mastered the study of common sense. That's okay, nothing really lost, but time. And at twenty, nine months was not too much time lost.

It was my sophomore year when I officially met Jay Davis. I had a lot to prove being the lead majorette, so I use to work on our routines religiously in a dance room in the main gym. It was not too far from the weight room and people were always passing by. I had been working on this routine pretty hard and had finally gotten it the way I wanted it to be done. When I finished, I heard clapping and turned around to see Mr. Fine. That's the nickname the girls on campus called Jay. He is about six feet tall and black as charcoal. He has the perfect shaped head that he keeps totally hairless by choice. Not only is his face chiseled, but he has nice muscles, not too bulky, but just right. His smile drives women crazy. He has beautiful white teeth and perfectly shaped full lips. His legs are strong and bowed. It was hard not to be one of his conquests, but there was something about him that would not allow me to let myself go all out for him.

We hit it off immediately. He was the kind of guy that kept you laughing and engaged with him wherever you were. I heard rumors about him and the girls on campus, but I never had real evidence of him cheating. He would always be with me and was always holding my hand or had his arm around me. All his friends referenced me as his girl, so I had no real reason to think he was messing around.

One night I had a lot of studying to do and could not make it to his fraternities' set they were having at their house. I had an exam the next day that I needed to prepare for. After studying a few hours and feeling more confident about the information, I decided to take a break. Nikki was itching to get over to the frat house, so we decided to go by. It was not an all-out party, but there were enough people there that I had to look for Jay. When I went upstairs to one of the rooms, I could hear a voice behind one of the doors that sounded like Jay's. I did not feel like I needed to knock, so when I opened the door Mr. Davis had some girl bent over the bed and was enjoying himself immensely. When he looked over and saw me, I calmly shook my head and walked away. Jay caught up to me outside buttoning his pants and trying to put on his shirt. He went into the whole it's not what you think routine. That bitch does not mean anything to me. I don't even know her last name. Why a man thinks that by having sex with somebody they don't know the last name of makes the girl look bad and not them is a mystery to me. Since I was not in love with Jay, there was not a very emotional exchange. I explained to him calmly that he really needed to go back inside and find out what the girl's last name was he was just with, because as far as I could see she was the one that he needed to be talking to. It was over with us and I would not entertain any excuses or calls from him in the future. Of course, he called for several weeks, but when I'm done, *I'm done*.

Michael is ordering another round of drinks for the table. He advised me that glass of wine number two would be my limit for the night. I'm not sure if the attention he is giving me is so protective because he's a friend of the family, or something else. I'm also not sure if his arm is around my seat because the place is so crowded, and he has to lean in to hear me or because of some other reason. As a matter of fact, I'm not sure about much right now. All I know, is there is a chemistry brewing, and I can't tell if it's one sided or my wine is taking its toll. I do know that Michael is married, and he's married to my godmother. And no matter how I am feeling sitting so close to him that I can feel the warmth and sweetness of his breath, I would not dare give in to my thoughts for this man I know, who is a stranger.

Chapter Two

MICHAEL

What is baby girl doing at a sports bar with a glass of wine in her hand? I'm glad I can oblige her and her girl with a seat. I guess I had better keep an eye on her for Mack, Meeka's dad. That's the least I can do since he kept my last rendezvous quiet from my wife. Although Mack's wife, Linda, is my wife's best friend, the male bond is still alive as ever. It starts out as innocent as always, but I can't seem to keep away from the ladies. It just so happened Mack was with me that night at the boxing match at David's. Denise was hot as ever and she was all over me. Mack seemed to be cool with me dropping him off at the house on my way to the hotel with Denise. He never mentioned it and neither did I.

Mack and I have what you would call a forced friendship. Since our wives have been best friends twenty years, they are very close. Mack is a good guy. He's probably not someone I would choose to hang out with, but we are definitely in each other's company quite frequently. He is a family man and does the whole church, stay at home routine. I admire his commitment to his marriage relationship, although I would appreciate it if he could keep his wife in her own marriage and out of mine. I can't stand his wife. She is constantly bad mouthing me to my wife and trying to give her two cents into our problems. I understand friendship, but Linda crosses the line. I think I've finally made her feel uncomfortable enough to keep her out of my home so much, but she's also a phone gabber. I think she and Diane spend most days gossiping on the phone about crap nobody cares about. Mack loves his one and only daughter, Meeka.

He seems to be a great dad; I always wondered why they stopped with just one kid—probably because Linda worried the hell out him during her pregnancy.

Diane has told me on multiple occasions that Meeka is her dad's heart and that it is a sore spot with Linda—whatever Meeka wants her dad ensures that she gets it.

I think Linda would prefer to see a little work out of Meeka, especially since Mack sides with Meeka on most mother/daughter disagreements. On any given day of the week, Diane and I are acting out the happy couple role with Mack and Linda.

It's not that I don't care for my wife, but the home life was not what I envisioned it to be. Diane came into my life at a point where I wanted to be a different man. I felt it was time to settle down and stabilize. I had been pretty wild all during my teen years and early twenties. I believed women were prey and I was the great hunter. Although I never had to hunt much, they always seemed to fall in my lap. I knew right up until the marriage ceremony that I should not marry this woman, but I thought she could be the influence I needed to change my ways. Well, let's just say change comes from the inside and not from outside.

I met Diane during a marketing event her firm put on after hours at my office. The partners at Ferguson & Smith Engineering were thinking about expanding globally. We had been searching for a marketing firm to support our vision. Several firms had either hosted us for lunch or dinner to make their pitch. Diane's company actually catered a late dinner and drinks at our office under the guise of understanding how much time we spend at the office.

Diane made the introductory pitch and afterwards, several of her colleagues navigated the room to answer specific questions that we may have had. I eventually connected with Diane, and we talked extensively about my role at F&S. I am very passionate about my career and have completed major projects during my tenure at the firm. There are water cooler comments about me making partner soon.

I really liked Diane's professionalism and her conversation. I could not tell if she was checking me out like most women do until the conversation turned personal. She mentioned she did not have time to pour into a relationship with her job and teenage daughter. I did not shy away from the fact she had a teenage daughter. It was almost a plus, since so many women want to have a child and I don't. I liked what I was seeing and hearing, so I turned on my charm.

As soon as I saw her nipples go hard behind the silk blouse she was wearing, I knew she was checking me out.

Meeka is cute and so is her friend Nikki, but there is something a bit more special about baby girl. I think it's because she is gorgeous and does not try and use it to her advantage. She is so damned serious and focused to be just twenty.

If I did not know Mack and Linda, I'd guess she was Puerto Rican. She's got long soft hair that lands above the small of her back. Her skin is spotless and reminds me of the color of sand in the Bahamas. At 5'7, she is slim with a nice tight body. If it was not for her nice butt, she would be too skinny. Some guys like feet, I do to; but I'm a sucker for pretty teeth and nice gums. I know too it sounds crazy, but when I'm kissing a woman, or she's giving me head, I want to know she has a healthy mouth. That's just the way I am. Meeka's mouth is beautiful. Her teeth are white and flawless with pretty pink gums. Either she has taken great care of her teeth, or Mack has spent a fortune in dental work. I've never taken the time to really talk with her, but she has good conversation. She's open and honest, and her smile is captivating me. I like the way she leans her head over to the side when she's laughing. Her eyes are really dark and complimented by the longest, thickest eyelashes I've ever seen. I wonder how you can be around someone for four years and not really notice them until all of a sudden. ~yunde.

I typically don't take ~~take~~ use any of my time listening to a woman talk about another guy, but Meeka has no problem expressing herself. She's confident and deliberate in what she has to say, so hearing her talk about her breakup with Jay really helps me understand her more. Most women are ashamed to admit that their man was messing around on them. I think it's a slight to their ego, but Meeka does not see it that way. I can't hate on Jay, at twenty, I would have been doing the same thing.

I'm thirty and still can't keep myself under control.

I am intrigued at Meeka's ability to maintain her virginity—especially since she is drop dead gorgeous. I've seen her dance at a few games and although I was not really checking her out, I could not miss the way she shakes that body.

The girl can move her body and mesmerize you with those curves.

I'm sure every little punk on campus has made it a mission to be the first to hit that, so I'm sure it has not been easy for her. I can't help but imagine how nice it would be to be the first and only man to take little Miss Meeka to ecstasy.

I don't normally connect with women on any level other than sexual, mainly because I am married and only looking for a good time. However, sitting here talking with Meeka is peaking much more than the need for sex. With me being an engineer and her studies in architectural engineering, it allows her to understand what I'm talking about relative to my *career* job. She's really into sports and understands the game of football very well. I like that. I spend a lot of time and money in sports related activities. I've got five thousand dollars on tonight's game. But most of all, her sweetness is the most attractive thing about her. In over an hour, she has yet to say one negative thing. She's sincere when she laughs. She's not just giggling at everything I'm saying. I know I was not this together at twenty. They do say women mature much faster than the brothers.

The sports bar is kind of loud and Meeka is soft spoken, so I have to lean in closer to hear her. As I slide closer to her and lean in, I can smell her. Her scent is driving me wild. It's not a heavy perfumed smell, but more of a natural clean smell. I'm not sure of the wine she is drinking, but I want to taste her lips so bad. Whenever she takes a sip, she darts her tongue around her moist lips and my imagination immediately gives me other ideas about her mouth.

I can't believe I'm even thinking this way about this girl. I've never messed around with a woman ten years my junior. Not that I go around checking identification, but the women I've been with in the past are either my age or older. I'm not one of those guys that get off on having a younger woman. I guess that won't happen until I'm in my forties or fifties. I've always preferred older women. Nothing annoys me more than being around an immature female. The whining and the neediness is a quick turn off. Diane was just the opposite. Unfortunately, she was just a little too independent and that started to turn me off. I can tell Meeka is not like that. Even when I've been around her in other settings, she has always carried herself like a classy lady. The only thing that has ever really reminded me of her age is when others refer to her as Diane's goddaughter.

Perfect example of how mature this girl is. Most women have to go to the lady's room in twos, but she does not even give Nikki a glance when she asks to excuse herself to run to the restroom.

I'm trying to get a hold of myself.

This is one prey that I don't want to land in my lap.

It would be total chaos if I tried to sleep with my wife's goddaughter. Mack would try and kill me if I hit on his virgin daughter. I'm not crazy, but I'm definitely interested. I think she is feeling something to. David's eyeing me like, motherfucka I know you ain't that crazy. Before I know it, I'm headed towards the restroom myself. I meet Meeka in the passageway and ask her if she's okay. There's that smile and those pretty teeth. I know I should not do this, but as I slide my hands around her waist and pull her up against me, I think about what I'm doing and what some of the consequences might be. I lean towards her and kiss her gently because I don't want to frighten her, but I want her to know what I'm feeling.

Her soft moist tongue meets mine and I can taste her innocence.

This is a different kind of kiss, a different kind of response. I've had a lot of women, but there is something different with Meeka. As we pull apart, I can tell in her eyes she's vacillating between feeling good and feeling guilty. I am to, but not about being married, it's about wanting more with Meeka. I ask her who drove to the sports bar, and she told me she rode with Nikki. I wanted to spend more time with her to explore what I was feeling, so she agreed to let me take her back to the dorm.

When we got back to the table, I tried to act like nothing had happened, but I'm sure David could tell that I had crossed the line. I did not feel awkward at all sitting next to her and focusing every ounce of attention her way. The game was the last thing on my mind. I don't think I had turned back to the tv monitors since Meeka joined our table. David had to tell me I won when the game ended.

We left the sports bar around 11:00pm and walked to my car. I'm a Lexus man and for me there is no other color than black. I like the finer things in life. Nice place to call home, nice cars and beautiful women; top that off with some cognac and I'm pretty cool. Money has never been an issue for me. We were not rich, but my folks had enough sense to save up for college. There was not a lot of extra, so I picked up the habit of gambling. The good news is I win more than I lose. The bad news is, I've been gambling for a while and I'm not really interested in stopping. I play cards in town, usually on Friday nights. I'm good to win anywhere from $5k to $7k a sitting. I bet big on football and usually make a trip to Vegas every other month. I rarely touch the six figures I make as an engineer, so it's practically impossible for anyone, including my wife to know where my money is going. I only lay bets on what I can pay off when and if I lose. It took one time in college for me to learn that lesson quickly.

I really needed to make some fast cash and I knew I had a sure win on a game. I bet two thousand dollars with a bookie I knew and I only had about five hundred. At the end of the game, my team had lost by only a touchdown. The game went down to the wire and I was sweating bullets. When the game was over and my team had lost, I was sick as a dog. I knew there was no way I could go to my Pops and get the money.

After a couple of days, my phone was ringing off the hook. The messages went from "where is my money," to "punk I'm looking for you." One night David and I were out and from nowhere these two big dudes rolled down on us and beat the hell out of me. I did not really blame David for staying down. He tried to help, but it was really no use in both of us taking a beating. I had two days to come up with the money or body parts were going to start missing off me. This is where the rubber hits the road on true friendship. David took part of his scholarship money, which was supposed to be for books and paid my debt off. In a couple of weeks, I won the money back, but I had learned a valuable lesson.

I don't like getting beat down.

As I escort Meeka into the front seat of my car, I lean in to buckle her seatbelt for her. I can't help but want to taste those sweet lips once more to make sure that what I was feeling is truly worth the trouble that I may get myself into. I intentionally pause after the seatbelt snaps and brush my lips against hers. Again, I know I've kissed over a hundred women, why is this girl's taste so good? With one hand bracing myself against the seat, I gently put the other around her neck. Her skin is so soft and I can control our kissing with my hand. I feel her the moan in her throat, and I know that she is into this as much as I am. I don't know where this is going to lead, but I need to get her back to the dorm. I'm not rushing anything with this much at stake.

Being with Meeka, in the car on the way back to her dorm, feels very familiar and comfortable. I can't really describe it, but it's like I'm in the right place, at the right time, with the right woman. I rest my hand on her thigh against her jeans.

"Baby girl are you alright". I keep asking her is she okay, partly because I want to make sure she is and partly because I want to make sure I am not misinterpreting things.

"I'm fine Michael; I should be asking you are you okay. It seems like things are happening really fast here and I'm kind of in an emotional daze right now. I really don't want to hurt anybody, but I can't seem to control the way I am feeling." I tell her I'm fine and let's just consider ourselves exploring these newfound feelings. I don't plan to rush anything. I know that this is a very delicate situation we are putting ourselves in.

When we pull up to her dorm, I unsnap her seat belt and go around to open her door. Instinctively, I pull her into my arms and place a kiss against her lips. This time, I'm not as gentle I want her to know my desire for her. I palm her waist with my hands and let my tongue express all my feelings. I want this girl in a bad way.

Chapter Three

MEEKA

I can't believe Nikki beat me back to the dorm room. She must have left right after we did and left alone. I know she's probably disappointed, but at least her hot tail is safe and sound. I think David was being a nice guy but was not interested in Nikki. She was practically in his lap all night long. Sometimes I wonder how this girl even stays in school with the men chasing she does. But I can say one thing, she has perfect girlfriend ears. I have got to tell her about Mr. Michael and all these crazy sinful feelings I'm having about this very married man. I would not have guessed in a million years that I would get involved with a married man, especially my godmother's husband. What does that say about me, what does that say about Michael?

"Hey girl, I see that you made it back safe and sound. Are you still a virgin?"

I know she did not just ask me that, like I would be giving it up to Michael the first night. "Yes, I am still a virgin. Are you?" Nikki did not have to answer; she just hiked up her butt and patted it at me.

"Sit down and tell me all about that fine man you were all up on tonight. I have to give it to you

Dialogue

Meeka, he is definitely cute. This is one night; I would have been making love for sure. No way I would be back in this dorm room this early after leaving with hazel eyes. I know he was feeling you because I don't think he stopped gazing at you for one second. If he had licked his lips one more time, I would have jumped across that table and start kissing him myself. When he got up to go to the restroom, the print in his jeans left no imagination that he is packing."

That's one thing I can say about Nikki, whatever she is thinking, she will say.

I noticed Michael was well endowed when he pulled me close to him outside the restroom. Don't get me wrong, I know what a penis is, I just have not been penetrated with one. However, I think tonight was the first night I really could have seriously considered it.

"Okay, Nikki, listen. I have such mixed emotions going on right now. I enjoyed tonight with Michael. He's cute, attentive, funny, and sexy; but he's so married. I want to spend more time with him, but I can't let myself stoop that low to be with someone that is married. This would devastate my mother's relationship to Diane, and my relationship with my mother and godmother. My dad would be totally pissed. I don't know what he would do to Michael. I don't think I've ever heard of someone falling for their godmother's husband."

"Bitch, calm down! That's your problem Meeka; you evaluate things too damn much. You are twenty years old and so uptight. Why don't you just ride this wave out and see what happens. You and Michael might hook up again, go out and find that tonight was some kind of fluke. No real harm done, but at least you took a chance on an emotion without evaluating it to death. Michael is a grown man; he should be committed to his wife, not you. He stood up and married her, not you. He has to lie in bed with her, not you." Nikki was right in a way, but I still felt a little eerie about what was happening.

I could not imagine a happy ending to what has started either way.

If it was a fluke, I would always feel awkward around Michael and Diane going forward. If I allowed this to progress and I developed irretrievable feelings for Michael, I could be deeply hurt if he ended a relationship with me. If we fell in love and we ended up together, what would that do to our families?

"Meeka to earth. I bet you are evaluating right now. Well, evaluate this. If you don't give this a chance, and you come back to the room one night and Michael is making love to me, don't be mad. I mean you're my girl and all, but I am not a fool. Michael was dropping cash like a gum wrapper to the ground. I saw you guys pull off in that Lexus and I know for a fact that he had more damn designer on that Neiman's carries. I won't think twice about godmother Diane." Sometimes I wish I could be as ruthless as Nikki, but that just would not be me. I've always cared too much. Although Nikki tries to be *hard*, I do know she can be vulnerable to love too. I remember when she dated Ray. He was a police officer and about five years her senior. They had been seeing each other for a few months and she was head over heels for ~~Ray~~ Bryan. One night we had been hanging out and she could not reach him on his day off. She convinced me to drive her over to his apartment complex. She did not want to use her car in case he saw her stalking him. His personal car and patrol car were both parked in front of his apartment. I tried to convince her not to knock on his door unannounced. Something told me he was up to no good. Nikki knocked on the door and he finally answered. There was another woman standing behind him and he pretty much blew Nikki off. As she walked back to the car, I could tell she was so hurt. I wish I was gutsy enough to give him a piece of my mind but after Nikki keyed his personal car and the patrol car, I think enough had been done. I could tell for the next week though that she was really affected by how he treated her.

After I finished telling Nikki about Michael's wonderful kissing skills, I got dressed for bed. I knew exactly what I would be dreaming about tonight and a soft smile came over my face.

Chapter Four

MICHAEL

I should have known Diane would still be up. There really should be no nagging tonight. It's only midnight and she saw David leave with me for the sports bar. David's car was being serviced and he had reserved a loaner vehicle. He asked me to swing by the BMW dealership and scoop him up. I needed to swing by my house to change before we headed out, I'm glad my boy was able to give him a lift back, so I could take Meeka home. Regardless, it would have been better if she was in bed.

Immediately after our marriage, things started going downhill. The same things that attracted me to her from the jump became an instant turn off. I thought that her strength and independence was an admirable trait. I know she raised her daughter single handedly after her boyfriend, at the time, split. That would make any woman strong. She finished college and landed a decent job at a marketing firm. She handled her business well and took care of herself physically. When we were dating and something broke, she would opt to call a repairman versus ask me to fix shit. I thought she was proactive and on top of her game. That got old quick. A man wants to feel like he is needed by his woman. I don't want a woman with all the answers. Don't get me wrong, I don't want a dumb blond, but I want a woman that values her man's thoughts, caters to what he wants her to do, feels a little lost if he's not providing her direction.

Diane really does not need me—she just thinks she does.

She enjoys my bedroom skills and likes to "have" a man, but if I were gone today, she would be okay. I think the more I cheat the more she is determined to have the perfect marriage and fix everything that is wrong. I'm not intentionally trying to mess up my marriage, but I'm just not in love with my wife.

I'm no fool either.

No need to run to nothing.

I mean, the women I screw around with are not women I would want to be with long term either. So, I have not been hard pressed to separate. Diane keeps a nice home for us, cooks well and is guaranteed loving. But when she starts running off at the mouth, a brother could catch a case if he did everything that he *thought* about doing. The last thing I want to do is hurt Diane. She is a good woman and deserves so much more; I just don't think I'm the one to give it to her anymore.

"Hi, did your team win tonight?" Diane is lying on the couch watching a movie. I have to give it to her she is definitely an attractive woman. She wears what I believe is called a bob, I call it a mushroom. She's about 5'9. She has a nice copper complexion. When we first met, I could not get enough of her. I'm not into big butts, but I like enough to keep me busy. People sometimes mistake us for sister and brother because of our eyes. She has more of a brown tint versus the green in my eyes, but they stand out enough to get your attention. If I liked kids, and I don't, we would have made some pretty babies together. Her daughter, Diamond, is off at college, out of state, thank goodness. Interestingly enough, Diamond is Meeka's age and I believe that they were good friends in high school. Diamond was probably to ghetto for Meeka to continue to hang around. I was glad she left for college a couple of years after I married her mother. I was sure some of my stuff was going to come up missing with those little thugs she brought home. Diane wanted me to play more of a dad role in Diamonds life. If I don't want my own kids, I was not about to play dad to someone else's. With Diamond being a teenager, I definitely did not want to play that role in her life. I've had to correct a few of her male friends when she brought them home, but that was more for me and how I wanted things to run in my house.

Having two women in the same house, constantly arguing, was a nightmare.

Diamond can be pretty disrespectful to her mom, and in all honesty, Diane can be very controlling. I stayed out of it and away from it as much as possible.

"Yes, my team won. Anything in the fridge to munch on?" She jumped up and went into the kitchen to get me some hot wings she had fixed earlier. This is the kind of thing that makes me feel bad about my little excursions, but what can a brother do.

"Honey, do you want to go to the game tomorrow? Linda has four tickets. Meeka left them for her earlier this week and I thought it would be nice to get out and I can see my goddaughter shake her groove thing." Hell naw. I am not about to sit up at a football game with Diane watching Meeka shake that fine butt of hers while I'm dreaming about getting a piece of it soon. I've been having thoughts about her all the way home. The last kiss of the night gave me much to think about. This girl brings out something in me that is much different than I've felt in a long time. As a matter of fact, I don't really recall having these feelings before. She has such a sweet nature about her that you can't help but want to be around her. When I plugged her number into my phone, I was actually hoping we could connect tomorrow or shall I say today since it's after midnight. I did not think to ask if she had a game to perform at today and I guess she did not think to tell me.

"Look Diane, I don't think I want to go to the game tomorrow. I need to catch up on some work and get some rest."

"Michael, you act like you can't do anything with me. Every time I ask for you to spend time with me, it seems as if you always have something else to do."

"Don't start with that every time shit Diane. I don't won't to go to the damn game. Let's not make a big deal out of it." I knew the nagging would start eventually.

"Maybe if I were one of those ho's you were out screwing, then you would have time to do something with me. Maybe if I were a damn deck of cards, you would have time. I'm tired of this Michael, you do what you want to do, but it's never with me. How do you think things are ever going to get better if you are not ever planning on trying to make them better?"

How does a motherfucking football game turn into making our marriage better? Diane can mess a night up quick. "Look, if you want to go to the damn game, then fine. I'll go to the game." I left it at that and went upstairs.

I suddenly lost my appetite and jumped in the shower, thought about Meeka the entire time. Even when I brushed my teeth, I thought about her. Later on, when I got in the bed, I made love to Diane wishing she were Meeka the whole time.

Chapter Five

MICHAEL

I was on my way to shoot some hoops and get my Saturday exercise, so I figured I'd give baby girl a call. For the past two years every Saturday, me and some of the fellas meet up at the gym to shoot ball. We normally play for a couple of hours and then break. I'm fanatical about staying in shape and shooting ball helps me do that. It is also a way I can burn off stress. I dialed her number, and it rang a few times before she answered.

"Hey baby, are you up and about?" Immediately, I started trying to figure out a way to see her. I had to taste those lips this morning.

"Hi Michael, I'm glad you called. I was thinking about you and was hoping to hear from you today".

"I tell you what sweetheart, you can do more than just hear from me if you like today". I could feel her smiling through the phone. She paused for a moment and said she would love to see me, but she has a performance at 2:00pm and had to be at the stadium by Noon. It was already 10:00 o'clock, so I asked her to meet me at the gym.

"Michael, I don't think that's a good idea. I'm already uncomfortable about you being married. I don't want anyone to know that I'm interested in you".

"Sweetheart, no one at this gym is going to know or care about you seeing me. I'm not going to make a scene; I just need to see you. I had you on my mind all last night and if I don't get a glance at you this morning, I'm going to go crazy." It was dead silence, I could tell she was really considering it, but was holding back on me. "You're not trying to make me beg baby girl are you?"

"Ok, I'll come by on my way to the stadium". I told her where it was and she said she would see me in a few.

I'm no Allen Iverson, but I can hold my own on the court. We were a few minutes into the second game when I noticed the guy's attention was directed elsewhere. You can always tell when a fine woman enters the gym, especially one that is new to the scene. Several of the girlfriends of the guys come by every Saturday. I'm not sure if they like to watch us play or just make sure their man is only playing ball.

Sherry is here. A while back, one of the other girlfriends brought this cute chick Sherry to watch us play. My screw antenna immediately went up. She is fine, but with two small kids it just was not working for me. She gave me all the head I could stand, but when I called and heard those damned kids in the background, I just could not bear it. I think she wanted more than I could give anyway.

Why when a man is upfront about being married, not leaving his wife, and definitely not wanting kids; women go superwoman on him?

Like this is the challenge they have been waiting for and make it their mission to change the man's mind. When she finally realized I was serious about not being serious with her, she had the nerve to get pissed. This woman threatened to call Diane, said she had pictures of us in bed and was going to make sure Diane had them for the divorce trial and everything.

Things got crazy that night.

I don't normally hit women, but the record needed to be set straight that I was not one to threaten. I gave her a full 90-day money back guaranteed spanking. I'm glad her kids were with their dad for the weekend, because the lesson on do not threaten was taught that night. Believe it or not, I still hooked up with her a few times after that. I believe I turned her on more after I smacked her around than before. Go figure.

Meeka had these short dark blue workout shorts on, with a tee shirt that showed her flat stomach and sexy navel. She had on flip flops with her toenails polished in red. On any other girl, that would have just been sports gear. On Meeka, it was sexy as lingerie. I had taken my shirt off and was sweating pretty heavily. I called time out and grabbed my towel to wipe my face and six pack abs off. I could feel Sherry drooling. She always said she loved when I sweated and the hairs below my navel lay down.

As I walked towards Meeka, I thought what the hell. I really missed this girl since last night. I could tell in her eyes she was still feeling me as well. I leaned over and gave her a kiss on the mouth and quickly darted my tongue in and out as I grabbed her bottom lip gently with my teeth. Man, she tasted good. This girl instantly turns me on. It's going to be difficult to pace this relationship. She took a deep breath and looked totally embarrassed.

"Michael, you can't go around doing that." All the while she was grinning and blushing ear to ear.

"Sweetheart, I can't help myself. When I'm near you I want you." She ran her fingers through her hair—which I noticed being the astute gambler I am—is a tell-tale sign of hers when she is a little nervous or uncomfortable. I asked her where she parked and told the guys that I'd be back in fifteen minutes. The hole that was burning in my back from Sherry's glare was annoying the hell out of me. I guess she forgot I was not her man.

"So, tell me what I should expect from the performance this afternoon." Meeka looked surprised.

"Are you coming to the game?"

"Yep." I was hoping she did not ask me who with. For some reason, Meeka was not someone I wanted to start lying to.

"Who are you coming with?"

I knew she would ask. "Who did you give those four tickets to?"

"I gave them to my parents a week or so ago, I guess my mother invited Diane."

I did not like that look on her face. The last thing I want to do right now is push her away from me. "Baby listen, I don't have to come to the game. I don't want you to feel uneasy in anyway. I'm trying to sort through this myself. All I know is I'm constantly thinking about you and I'm not willing to stop the forward motion here. I know that sounds pretty bad coming from a married man, but I'm sharing my true feelings with you right now Meeka."

"I feel the same way, but I'm scared at what's going to happen as we continue moving forward. What if...?" I stopped her right there and told her let's take one step at a time and let the cards fall where they may.

I could tell she had just showered, so I held back my desire to pull her close. When we reached her car, I told her if I did not see her tonight after the game I'd see her early in the week. Nice, this time she popped up on her toes and slid her sweet tongue into my mouth. I could tell she was a dancer by the way she balanced herself without falling into my sweaty chest. Her initiated kiss was clean and perfect. It did not seem like a repeat rehearsal like some women who kiss all the time. Meeka had a pure kind of kiss, and I liked it. I patted her on the backside and told her I'd see her in a bit. When she drove off, I was feeling pretty good. Then I turned around and damned near knocked Sherry over, I was put on edge.

"So, is Miss Thang the flavor of the month?"

I told Sherry to back up and stay away from me. Just like a jealous woman she is running off at the mouth about how I'm into jailbait. I walked back into the gym thinking how did I ever find her attractive?

I finished up the basketball game, showered and went home to get Diane. We sat through the game and half time with no major action. Diane did mention that my binoculars were getting the best of me during half time. I had this very interesting emotion—some call it jealousy. As I was checking out Meeka during half time, I noticed a lot of other men had their binoculars focused on the field as well. The idea of this many men staring at Meeka and seeing the same bouncing and jiggling tits that I saw and was yearning for had the green-eyed monster on alert in me. I'm not normally a jealous guy. That emotion left shortly after college, so for it to be happening now felt strange. There was nothing I could really do about it in the near term, but Meeka and I would have to have a discussion about this dancing at some point.

I laid low for the rest of the weekend. I was able to chat with Meeka briefly on Sunday, but with church for her and a lot of studying the phone was all we could do. I liked the fact the Meeka was into church and found it important to go. I hope this would not become a sore spot in our relationship as it has with Diane.

I believe in God and had gone to church in my younger days.

I hate it when people want to box you into what they think you should do to display your belief—Diane used to nag me constantly about going to church. In one argument, I came close to naming all the women in her church that I either screwed, or who had wanted me to screw them. I did not want to crush her faith like that.

I planted myself on the couch watched some football and prepared for a grueling work week.

Chapter Six

Meeka

It's been three weeks and Michael and I have been spending quite a bit of time together. It's hard to believe he's married. After he gets off of work, we go to dinner, or he even has come up to my dorm a few times. I say a few times because Michael says he's a grown man and coming to the dorm does not do much for him. Since it's been pleasant out, we meet for lunch and sit outside at a park near his office and talk. I'm still amazed at how much we have in common. We can talk endlessly and he's passionate about his interests, just as I am about mine.

He called me one time around two o'clock in the morning. He said he was just finishing up a card game and wanted to see me. I know I should not have done that, but I can never seem to say no to that man. I was so groggy, but I still agreed. He was starving, so he picked me up to go to breakfast. There was no way I was eating that early in the morning. We ended up at an all-night restaurant. Michael amazes me with how comfortable he is with me while out in public. The place was relative busy for that time of the morning. When we got there, Michael had spoken to a few of the other patrons. I felt awkward that he knew some of the people there, but Michael did not seem to let it faze him. As I sat down in the booth, Michael slid in right beside me. Before I could protest, he began to passionately kiss me. Even though I'm always so nervous in public, I can't push him away. He is so caring and affectionate towards me. I can't help to be blown away by him.

This is not the Michael I hear my mother talking about. She never has anything good to say about him. She was telling my dad that Diane is convinced he's fooling around again. He is back to his no show and no care attitude. My mother says that Diane is distraught more so this time because she believes Michael has feelings for this heifer. I'm not sure how she came to that conclusion, but it actually made me feel good to know that I was different in his eyes. I don't go anywhere near Diane. At this point, I'm so wrapped up in Michael that I can't stop this train if I wanted to. I feel so good when I am with him. He has a way of making me feel safe and protected. He is so confident that I know he can handle anything that we have to face. It's still hard for me to believe I'm involved with a married man. I've never been the type of person to do anything outside of what I believed was morally or ethically right. I was raised in the church and both my parents have always taught me to respect other people. Their marriage has been the role model for what I want for my own life. I know I should be stronger, but with Michael I have no control.

Other than kissing and caressing, Michael does not pressure me for sex. I wish he would. I truly believe he is the man that I've been waiting to give myself to. When I mentioned to him, that I wanted to be with him, he said he plans on taking his time with me. In one recent conversation, he wanted to know specifically what I have experienced sexually and with whom. I'm very open with him and was fine to answer the questions, but they seemed odd to me. He wanted to know if a man has ever touched my bare breast with his hand or tongue. I told him no.

He wanted to know if a man has ever seen me totally naked.

I told him no.

The furthest I've ever gone with a man was my ex, Jay. We would kiss and I allowed him to rub my breast through my top and we would grind some, but I just never felt comfortable, and it turned out that I should not have. If Michael needed to know this, for whatever reason, I was okay to tell him. He has also been very forthcoming with me. I asked about his affairs and if he wore protection every time. He said always. He has no intentions on fathering children or dying over being stupid. He agreed that when the time came he would be more than willing to take an AIDS test together. That's important to me. The last thing I want to do is to get a deadly disease after waiting so long to make love. I'm constantly hearing about females on campus having unprotected sex. Some of them getting pregnant, and others getting and giving diseases. You would think educated people would have enough sense to protect themselves and their mates. College life can be a lot of fun, but it can be as dangerous as being on streets if you don't use common sense.

When I got back to the dorm today, there were more roses waiting for me. Nikki has been fussing talking about this damn room ain't no conservatory. She is just jealous that Michael is romancing me. All the screwing she's done and I have yet to see a dandelion be delivered to this room for her. Michael even told me he did not want me asking my parents for another dime. He wanted me to come to him for all my needs. I told him that I did not feel comfortable with that arrangement, but he was adamant that he was not taking no for answer.

One day, Nikki and I were going shopping, so I called because I needed to get a few things. I went by the gym and he broke me off $500 dollars without blinking. I thought Nikki was going to crap in her pants. I told him I did not need that much money, but he simply said save it for later. When we got back to the car, Nikki kept saying I know you are screwing him. He would not be doing all this if he was not tapping that tail. I had to swear to her that we have not had sex yet. I'm not sure she was convinced, but I really did not care what she thought. My baby is good to me and I am stone crazy about that man.

Michael mentioned that David was going out of town on overnight business and he wanted us to spend some quality time together. Tonight after the game, I'm going to meet him at David's for the evening and who knows what will go down. Of the friend's I've met of Michael's, I really like David. I can tell they have a very strong brotherly bond. David is a couple years older than Michael and seems much more settled. They went to high school together and college. They remind me of Nikki and me, meaning Michael being more like Nik and me more like David. I guess what they say about opposites attract is true. I think I would be bored stiff with David. He's a good guy and all, but Michael's personality is so dynamic that I never know what to expect from him. With me being so predictable this is just new to me, and I like it. I've been to David's house a couple of times, and you can tell he is doing well for himself. He has a very nice bachelor pad. His home is brick, three levels and decorated tastefully. He's definitely a good catch. I see why his girlfriend is always around. She does not want to lose a good thing.

One Saturday Michael and I were out and about, he took me to this nice lingerie store. I just knew we were not going in. One because he was married, but also because guys normally don't want to shop for lingerie, they just want to see it on you. When we went in the salesperson was nice and asked what she could help us find, Michael told her that he wanted to replenish my entire lingerie wardrobe of panties and bra's. I politely pulled him over to the side and told him that he was crazy; since he had not seen my lingerie yet, how could he know it needed to be replenished. I do have some taste. He did not hesitate to respond and tell me that he wanted me to discard every panty and bra set that I owned. Even the one's I had on now. That way, when he does start making love to me, I'll never be able to tell him not to take off what he bought. Needless to say, $1,500 later I walked out with three bags full of "what Michael liked."

As I thought about my night with Michael at David's, I thought about his girlfriend Pam. It took a minute for her to warm up to me. I was not sure if it was because she knew Diane or just because she did not like me. Once we chatted, I realized it was neither. She can't stand Michael. She thinks Michael brings out the worst in her man and will eventually get David into trouble. Michael had said Pam is ready for marriage and he thinks that is the furthest thing from David's mind. He does not blame him; he wishes he had waited as well. However, I think the more Pam sees me with Michael and the less she sees Michael woman chasing it makes her more comfortable with both of us.

It's weird, but I never ask Michael what he tells Diane when he's with me. I feel like I'm invading her privacy. I don't think I'd feel the same way if I did not personally know her and care for her, but these are unusual circumstances. I also never speak too far out in the future about Michael and me because I guess I have this last layer of protection up that realizes he is not mine. I think he senses that as well because he is constantly reassuring me about his feelings for me.

I've got to get a new phone, the ringer volume on this thing sucks. "Hey, baby. I'm packing a few things and heading that way now. Are we staying at David's, or going out somewhere I need to know about?" I was trying to feel him out about tonight. I am so nervous. I'd hate to pack something sexy and he still wants to "take his time." I'll feel real forward. Then on the other hand, I don't want to disappoint him and not look the way he wants me to just in case.

Ummmm.

He said we are in for the night and he's cooking dinner now. Since we have not taken the AIDS test yet, I guess Michael has condoms. Just in case, I'll grab some from Nikki's stash. In the past, when I have daydreamed about having sex and losing my virginity, there has never been a face to the man I would share myself with. Now, that I have a face for that man, my imagination has been running wild over Michael. I am so attracted to him physically and emotionally. I know that with Michael all my expectations will be exceeded. Oh, my goodness, I may really be making love for the first time tonight.

Chapter Seven

MICHAEL

I don't think I've ever waited three days to have sex with a woman, let alone three weeks. Even now, I'm not sure if I'm ready to take the most precious thing that Meeka has to offer. She has messed my head completely up. Don't get me wrong, I want to taste every inch of her and feel her sweetness engulf me completely, but I also want much more with Meeka. I've had my share of virgins, but I was also young. I have a whole different perspective and appreciation of some innocent scamper as a more mature man.

The last thing I ever want to do is hurt Meeka Brown.

These past few weeks I've gotten to know her. Each detail she shares, each emotion we exchange I've grown to care for her more and more. I've got it bad for baby girl. All I want to do is protect her and take care of her. No other woman I've messed around with has ever made me think about ending things with Diane and moving on, but I can't help to think about what a future with Meeka would be like. After a long day and coming home to someone you truly love and want to spend time with is what I believe should be how a marriage works.

Diane and I have been at it for what seems like every night this week. She is accusing me of all kinds of shit—most of it right on target. I've come pretty close to moving out, but I've got to play things cool. There is no way Diane can find out about Meeka and me before I know for sure what my next move will be. It's been about ten days since I've had sex with Diane and that's a first. I know that's her key that I'm messing around, but she's right and wrong. Emotionally I have checked out, but actually I have not been sleeping with another woman. Even when I think I should sleep with Diane out of obligation, I just can't seem to get aroused with her anymore. On the other hand, when I just hear Meeka's voice; my soldier stands to attention.

I'm not Emeril or anything, but I can grill up some food when I have to. Although Meeka eats like a bird, I've got a nice little setup waiting for her. Salmon sautéed in my special sauce, twice baked potatoes and a spinach salad with raspberry dressing. To top it off, I've got a nice, chilled bottle of wine. Meeka has a two-drink maximum. Her little butt gets tipsy too quick, and I want her very cognizant of everything that happens between us tonight. Wine is not my drink of choice. I'm sipping on some cognac. I'm mellow since I've been sipping for a while. David has a nice collection of music, and his crib is real nice. I can't see taking Meeka to a hotel for a night like tonight. I hope she'll be comfortable here with me tonight.

Dinner was great and my baby seems really happy. She started out a little nervous as she was constantly running those fingers through her hair. We've moved over to the couch and I am gazing into those dancing eyes and seeing everything I want in a woman. "Baby girl, are you alright?" Her happiness is more than anything I want right now.

"I'm more than all right, but you seem to have something on your mind. Do you feel like sharing?"

"Actually, a lot has been on my mind lately. I've been thinking so much about us, that I can't seem to concentrate on anything else but you. I need you to understand Meeka that your family will never accept a relationship between the two of us. I'm not the boy next door that Mack would receive with open arms. Your mother probably thinks she knows more about me and my marriage than I do." I could tell nothing I was saying was shocking her, which is a good thing. But I needed her to understand what she was truly facing before we took this thing to another level. Hell, I don't think I'm a bad guy, but her parents would not agree.

"Michael, I think you underestimate my parent's trust and respect for my judgment. I'm twenty years old and have not given my parent's any grief. Not many parents can say they have a virgin daughter studying architectural engineering with a 4.0 GPA." I was glad to see him smiling.

"Baby girl, I understand all that, but keep it real. Mack has hung out alone with me a couple of times. He may not be one of my closest friends, but he's seen a side of me that I'm sure would concern any father." I did not want to tell Meeka about Diane calling Mack and Linda over one night when we got into a bad argument. I'm sure she didn't explain her role in provoking me to slap the hell out of her. It was only one time that they got involved because I made sure Diane knew that our business stays in our home. I know though that Linda would not hesitate to tell Meeka this to try and sway her away from me. "Meeka, I've been known to have a temper. I'm not sure if you already know this or not, but Diane and I got into it one night and she called your parents over. Diane had a bit much to drink while we were out. For some reason, alcohol seems to embolden her. She started on the other women argument. I let her rant until she began poking me in the forehead with that bony accusatory finger of hers. I let my temper get the best of me Mack had to cool me down, but the damage was already done. I'm not trying to justify hitting a woman, but the circumstances may not have ever been clearly explained to your parents. I would never hurt you, but as a father, Mack won't see it that way."

"No, I did not know that had happened. It does not scare me away from you. Michael, every single experience we've had together thus far has been wonderful. You are gentle and sweet to me and that's all I need to know. You don't have to be concerned about anyone turning me away from you, baby I want to be with you."

That's all I needed to hear. As my tongue entered her mouth, I wanted to get lost in her right then and there. This special gift was being presented to me and my desire to open it was full. She leaned her head over to the side and my tongue went straight for the nape of her neck. Damn, her skin is so soft. I leaned her back on the couch and traced my tongue down to the front of her chest. As I unbuttoned her top and popped the back of her bra, I could feel her breathing grow rapid. I'm not an artist, but Meeka's breast needed to be on somebody's portrait. They were firm and her nipples were standing perfectly up. I traced the outside of her nipple with my stiff tongue and gently massaged the other breast with my free hand.

She let out a slight moan and I knew I was doing my job.

It was evident to me that I had not had any loving in ten days, because I was rock hard. I can stroke for a long time, but I know with Meeka I would not be able to last that long. I worked my way down her body and concentrated on that cute navel I saw a few weeks ago. As soon as my hands hit the buttons on those jeans, baby girl tensed up on me. I took my tongue and traced my way back up to her mouth. I looked her in the eyes and asked her, "Do you trust me?"

"Yes, baby I trust you."

"I need you to relax and completely trust me, sweetheart." As I started kissing her again, she told me that she was a little scared. That's not what I wanted. When I make love to her for the first time, I want her to be so relaxed and so ready that there is not any doubt or fear in her.

"Meeka, I'm not going to penetrate you tonight. Do you trust me?"

"Yes."

With that I picked her up and took her to the guest bedroom, I laid her on the bed and kissed her gently. I caressed her breasts and sucked her sweet nipples some more, all the while I was removing her jeans. I've been with a lot of women, but Meeka had to be the most sensuous woman I've ever seen naked. I intentionally stepped away from her so that she could see me remove my shirt and my pants. The whole time I was looking in her eyes. I smiled and asked her, "Do you still trust me?" She told me she did with all her heart. As I parted her precious spot with my tongue, the taste drove me crazy. She was so juicy and sweet. The taste alone confirmed for me she was truly a virgin. My tongue found her clit and I gently stroked. When she relaxed the muscles in her butt, I knew she was enjoying her man.

"Meeka, this is so good girl."

"Oh baby, you make me feel so good. Mi......" When I first heard her start to chime my name, I slid my index figure inside her and continued to lick on her clit and finger her.

"Oh, Michael, oh Michael, ooooooohhhh don't stop baby, ooooh!"

I had to squeeze my soldier or I would have exploded with her. I'm too old to go out like that anymore. You know you taste good when you don't mind kissing your man after he's been eating you out.

"Michael baby, I'm ready. I want to please you too." I kissed her and told her she already does please me then we both fell asleep.

Chapter Eight

Meeka

"That motherfucka did what?" Nikki made me wait while she popped popcorn at 10:00am in the morning, so she could have some while I told her about Michael and our night together. I gave her all the sordid details and she was screaming the entire time. She could not believe how Michael had been towards me. She insists that he must be in love with me. Although we've never used those words, I definitely feel like I am falling in love with him, if I'm not already there. Towards the end of sharing my story, I moved my hair behind my ears. What did I do that for? Nikki went wild. "I know those are not diamond studs in your ears."

This morning Michael got up and fixed us a light breakfast. He's a good cook and very creative. He chopped up fresh fruit and made a vegetable omelet that was wonderful. When I first came to the table there was a small box. Call me crazy, but for a moment I thought it may have been a ring. Then I thought about how ridiculous that was. He is already married, and we've only been together a hot minute. Anyway, I was blown away by the earrings and immediately started crying. Michael gave me a sweet kiss and told me if I plan on crying every time he did something for me, then I'd better carry plenty of tissue.

My phone is ringing. "Hello".

It's mommy dearest.

"Hi Meeka, your dad and I have not heard from you in over a week. I miss you, what's been going on?"

I explained to my mother that I've been so busy studying and with dance practice that I have not had a chance to drop by. I hated that I was not able to see them at the game, but there was no way I was going to go near them since Diane and Michael were there. I was apprehensive with Michael being at the game with his wife. I was able to keep it together, but the thought of him sitting next to her and playing the husband role really bothered me. I know I do not have any rights to Michael, but I've grown so close to him. I did not tell him how I felt. I don't ever want him to think that I would try to back him into a corner to make choices he might not be ready to make. I resolved with myself early on that any choices that would have to be made at some point would be mine. Meaning, if I felt like things were never going to progress into something more, or things were completely out of control; I would own the choices that would need to be made. I remember Nikki telling me that her sister had been involved with a married man for six years. She had tried to convince her sister that this guy was never going to leave his wife for her. Her sister was just too in love to let go. She eventually got pregnant and when he cut her off, she was devastated. The messed-up thing was she went to his wife and the wife forgave him. The only thing she got after six years was a baby and late child support.

My mother commented that my dad can't believe that I have not called him to make a deposit into my checking account recently. With all the money Michael has been giving me and now putting into my account, I have not needed anything from my parents. The last time I checked I had over $5,000 in my account. I have never had that much money and I don't really need it. I told Michael I'm frugal and he does not need to spoil me the way he does.

"Meeka, I forgot to tell you some great news. Your cousin Deena is getting married, and she wants you to dance at her wedding". The guy she's been dating this past year proposed to her. You know her mom has to throw her an engagement party. It's in two weeks. I want you to make every effort to attend. Although Deena is your second cousin, it's important for you to know your family members."

"Oh, that's great." Ever since I can remember I've been dancing. I took ballet and tap dancing every year of my existence. I've danced at so many weddings and church events I believe I am what you would call an amateur professional.

"Meeka, sometimes I hate that you are an only child because it means extended family is even more important and I know how you can be so private."

"Mom, I would not miss it for the world. I believe we don't have a game that Saturday; so that would be great. I don't think I ever met the guy she is marrying. What is his name?"

"His name is Todd." He's a really nice guy and she seems so excited and in love. I can't wait until you meet Mr. Right. How's Jay?"

"I guess he's fine. Don't forget we broke up."

"Meeka, he seemed like such a nice guy for you. He came from really good parents and was always so mannerable. You even told me he was supportive of your decision to maintain your virginity. You never said what happened."

"Mom, it's over and I really don't want to go into detail about it."

"Ok, ok, ok. Please try and get by this week. I really would like to see you. By the way, have you talked to your godmother?"

"No."

"Well honey, give her a call. She's going through a lot with that asshole husband of hers and I'm sure she would love to hear from you. Michael has her so stressed out, that I don't think she knows if she is coming or going. I talked to her early this morning around 8:00am to see if she wanted to go shopping and you know he was not even at home. I wish she would get rid of him. I hate to see him coming because I have to put on a fake act to stomach him."

"Mom, you really should stay out of their business. You are only hearing one side of things. You never know what's really going on. The times

I've been around Michael, he just does not seem like what you describe him as. I've heard that sometimes the husband in the marriage is portrayed as the bad guy, when in actuality, the wife is not really living up to what she should be doing either."

"Are you serious? He could not tell me a damn thing that would change my mind about him being a deadbeat. Diane has been committed to him since day one. I would know if she had ever stepped out on Michael. Hell, I think she should. I can't begin to count the number of times Diane has caught him cheating. The few times your dad has gone somewhere with him, I let Mack know that he had better not lose his freaking mind hanging around Michael."

"Ok, Nikki just came in and needs to talk to me. I love you and will get by soon. Give daddy a kiss."

"Bye, sweetie."

Nikki said I was going to have to pay her for using her all the time to dodge my parents. I hate lying to my mother, or anyone, but I can't sit through her bashing Michael. He is so right. I don't think my parents will ever approve of us having a relationship. My mom rarely ever curses, but something about Michael makes her loose her religion. This whole situation is so complicated.

I decided to get some studying done. With all the time I've been spending with Michael, I've slacked in my studies. I committed to myself I would study the remainder of the weekend, even if Mr. Johnson wanted to hook up.

Chapter Nine

MICHAEL

When I walked in the house, Diane was lying on the couch. It was after 10:00am and I could tell she had been crying and up all night. A guilty person comes in explaining. I went straight to the kitchen like I was starving. I started pulling out stuff to fix for breakfast. Diane came into the kitchen and wanted to know why I was just getting in. Even when I do stay out late playing cards, I normally am home before 3:00am and I at least have the decency to call. She wanted to know if I hated being married to her that bad that I could not even pick the phone up or answer her call.

"Diane look. I was not having a lucky night, so I stayed at the table. You know I just got that new phone with all the extra gadgets hooked up to it. It drains my battery real quick. I did not get your call. I had been drinking all night and I smoked a little weed. The game was over around 5:00am this morning and I laid on the couch and fell asleep." Cardinal rule #1, never let people know where you are illegally gambling. A mad spouse or jealous somebody could always send the cops there. Plus, in my case Diane might try to ride through. She knows that rule very well, so she did not expect me to tell her where I was. I don't think my answer made her feel any better as her eyes watered up.

"Michael, we need to get counseling. I don't know what to do to save our marriage."

I stopped long enough to look at her and I paused long enough to see that she was deeply hurting. She looked so tired, and I felt bad. I went over to her with the intent to hold her as I know that is what she really needed. When I put my arms around her, I felt the warmth of her body beneath the silk nightgown she had on. The least I could do was make her feel loved, even if I really didn't. This way, she would be satisfied and the ten-day drought I've been dragging around would be over. I raised her gown up and caressed her bottom. It felt as good as ever. I did not realize how much I needed to have sex, but I was more than ready. She was not Meeka, but I needed to be inside of her. After four years, I knew every inch of Diane's body and what made her feel good. It did not take long to hear her screaming my name and to relieve myself.

After I had sex with my wife, I laid around the house all day long. Both of those things seemed to have brought Diane some peace. A call came through at the house. It was the vendor that was working my last design preparing for production. They were having major problems and going live week after next was in jeopardy if they could not get the bugs out. I tried my best to talk him through it, but I was going to have to fly to Virginia first thing Monday morning. Typically, these types of things took 3 to 4 days.

Monday morning, on my way to the airport, I stopped by the doctors to have the blood drawn for the AIDS test. I figured I would be out of town when the results came back, so I gave them Meeka's dorm address to send the results to. My cell rang.

"What's up frat?" This was my boy T. I had not heard from him in a couple of weeks, and I could tell he was excited about something.

"What can I do you for frat?"

"Mike, I went on and did it."

"Did what?"

"I asked ole girl to marry me, man."

"Oh, hell naw. Are you really joining the sea of unhappiness?"

"Brother, that's not how a best man is supposed to talk. I was calling to see if you would do me the honors?"

"You know I got your back brother. I'm glad for you two. I think ole girl is really nice." T had been dating Deena for about a year and I think she's a good catch for him. He has long since seen his player days and she brings out the best in my man. Better him than me. T and I had been good friends since college. He's always been the type of guy that was able to settle into whatever relationship he was in. He knows that it is not my style, but we have remained close despite our differences.

After I hung up with T, I called baby girl. We did not talk live over the weekend. We were only able to exchange a few voice mails. She was in lockdown mode studying and I was just in lockdown mode period.

"Hey, sweetheart."

"Hi baby, are you on your way to work?"

"Yes, I did not want to leave this on your voicemail, but I've got to go to Virginia this morning on business. I'm heading to the airport now. Hopefully, I'll be back by the end of the week.

"Baby, what am I going to do a whole week away from you? I'm going to miss you." I'm not a soft type of brother, but I like the way Meeka talks to me. She makes me feel like I am the only man for her. I plan on keeping it that way too.

"I'll call you every night. It will go faster than you think. By the way, I took the test, and I had the results sent to you since I will be away. So, be on the lookout for them."

"Ok, are you sure you don't want me to take one to?"

"Do you think you need to take one? Did I miss something?"

"No silly, but I don't want to ask you to do something I would not."

"We're cool. I'll talk with you tonight.

It's the middle of the week and this design is not working. It never takes me this long to fix these types of issues. Half of the reason is that I can't really concentrate. I keep thinking about Meeka and wanting to see her. This hotel room is driving me crazy. I don't like to be cramped in like this. I called my assistant and told her to get a ticket to Virginia for first thing in the morning and a car to bring Meeka to the hotel. I've got to see that girl. My assistant wanted to be nosey, but she knows that I take good care of her and she had better always take good care of me. Which I have to admit she does. She's hid my indiscretions from Diane on more than one occasion with no questions asked.

I remember one close call when Diane decided to surprise me for lunch. One of my friends was already in my office and I had asked my assistant not to disturb me. I guess she knew I would be quite busy with Miss Stacey. Anyway, Diane wanted to wait and would have been sure to run into Stacey if she had hung around. My assistant was quick on her feet and talked Diane into taking her to lunch instead. When they left, she sent me a text message that Diane had come by and they were out to lunch. I was able to get Stacey out my office and back to work before my assistant and Diane returned.

"Meeka, I'm going to be here a couple of more days and I have got to see you baby". I was jonesing bad over this girl.

"I miss you too; I can't wait for you to get home".

"Listen, do you have any tests or anything you just can't miss tomorrow for school?"

"Ummm. No, not really."

"Ok, I've got you scheduled for a flight out first thing in the morning. A driver will pick you from the airport and bring you to my hotel. There will be a key waiting for you at the front desk." I was not asking any questions at this point. I don't believe in asking questions if there's only one answer I plan to accept.

"Michael, you want me to fly in for a one day trip? I'm sure this costs an arm and a leg. Plus, wouldn't it be better if I came in the afternoon when you got off from work?"

"No, I want you at the hotel when I get there, baby." I finished giving Meeka the logistics and started back to work. My focus was already improving as I knew within less than 24 hours, I would be holding my girl.

Chapter Ten

Meeka

I've only been to Virginia once when we took a trip to DC. I loved DC. It's one of those cities and areas with so much urban culture, yet so much history. I remember being intrigued by politics. DC almost made me decide on a different major for college. I could see myself as Olivia Pope running the quandaries of the political underworld. But even the architecture was so beautiful that my engineering mind could have done wonders there.

Who knows, maybe one day I may land in Chocolate City.

I'm glad Michael arranged for a driver because I would have been totally lost. I could tell in his voice that he really missed me. I have been going crazy without him, but I did not want him to worry about me. I packed a really nice number that I picked up earlier this week for him. I know he likes black, so the little, short nightie and panty set are just for him to enjoy. Since he passed his test, I guess tonight will be the night he makes me a woman. I have condoms so that no baby making occurs. Michael has been quite open about voicing the fact that he does not want children. I hope that's mainly because of the women that he has been with in the past.

Kids are everything to me.

I've wanted a large family ever since I could remember. I would not be happy short of four or five kids.

My parents tried to conceive more kids after I was born. My mother had endometriosis and was fortunate to be able to get pregnant with me. She was on bed rest for a few months and my dad was in a constant state of panic. I think the whole ordeal was more than they were willing to risk just to have another baby. I did not need to crave for attention, both my parents doted on me endlessly. I always wanted to have siblings to share my childhood with. There were times that I was overwhelmed with loneliness that could not be fulfilled with adult company.

I had a great childhood and really cannot complain.

I just know that is very important for me to be a mother and raise a family. There's not a baby I see that I could not just swallow up with affection and adoration. I don't think anything could change my mind about have children. It frightens me that it could be without Michael.

Chapter Eleven

MICHAEL

We finally worked out the glitches in this program. The configurations were off. I know I could have figured this out sooner if I was able to concentrate. We'll run a few more tests tomorrow to check the changes and make any additional adjustments. I can fly out of Virginia Friday morning. I need to make a run to Vegas this weekend. I'll drop my bags off at home, repack and head to Vegas late Friday night. I'm glad Meeka is here so we can spend some time together.

Meeka is in the room and I cannot wait to taste her sweet lips. It's amazing what a couple of months with someone can do to a man. My desire for her has grown more and more. I can barely get the door to my suite open when I am pounced on and smothered with the sweetest kisses from my baby. Her tongue tastes so good and she feels nice in my arms where she belongs. This is exactly the way a man should be greeted. I kick the door shut and with her legs wrapped around me I walk over to the bed. Damn I'm glad she's not a big girl, my back would have been broken. I think she knows instinctively that tonight is the night that I will be making love to her.

This outfit she has on is itching to be torn off her body.

I lay her on the bed and take off my suit jacket. Her pretty smile tells me all that I need to know about how much she missed me. As I start to kiss her, I realize how much I care about this girl. I also realize this feeling that I have for her is a new one for me. I'm undressing myself at the same time I'm kissing Meeka all over. Her lips, her breasts and her stomach are all so soft and are driving me crazy.

I have to taste her juices again.

My tongue slides around her special spot and I know she is ready for me. The wetness I felt as I slid her black panties off tells me she wants her man. It's going to take every ounce of control I have to be gentle. As I rub myself against her and began penetrating, Meeka is pushing my stomach back.

"Baby, you need to get a condom."

"Meeka, I'm not going to wear a condom this time sweetheart. It'll be okay." There was no way in hell I was going up in this innocence wearing a condom."

"Michael, please. We have to be careful."

"You trust me don't you?"

"Yes."

"Baby, I have to have you this way. Don't deprive me of that. I'm going to be the first and last man you will ever be with. I promise everything will be okay."

I went back to sucking her breast and heard her gently moan, "Ok".

As I entered her, I felt her nails go into my back and saw her eyes water up. I told her to relax and look at me. I kept my eyes locked on hers as I slid each inch of me inside of her. She was so tight that I did not think I would get it all in before I came. When I started stroking her, I could tell that she was no longer feeling as much pain but was thrusting back like she needed this just as much as I did.

"Meeka, you know you belong to me now?"

"Yes, baby."

"Tell me, girl."

"I belong to you, Michael."

"Tell me you will never let another man touch you."

"Michael, I'll never be with another man, but you…………..Mi…..ohhhhhhhhhhhhhh."

I would not have guessed she could get any tighter, but as she screamed my name, I would not have been able to pull out if I wanted to. She had me clamped so tight. I shared this perfect moment of ecstasy with her. The whole time with my eyes locked on hers.

"I love you, Meeka."

"I love you, Michael."

***

At dinner that night, I told Meeka about my boy T getting married and that I would be the best man. She asked me if she had ever met him, and I told her that he was at the sports bar the night we hooked up. His real name is Todd. She started panicking and asking who was he marrying and I told her a nice girl named Deena. What a coincidence, Deena is her cousin and Meeka is supposed to dance in the wedding. I thought the whole thing was funny, but Meeka was really upset about it. She did not think she could be in the same place with me and Diane. She was concerned that Todd would tell Diane or Deena about us. I assured her that men did not do things like that, especially my boys. She was planning to tell Deena that she would not be able to dance at the wedding. I told Meeka that was absurd and at some point we are all going to be in the same place together.

We talked about the engagement party coming up.

I wanted to reassure Meeka and let her know that I've juggled several women in the same place before, but I did not think that would be wise since we just made love for the first time. I also told her that I was popping in Friday and flying right back out to Vegas. I knew she had a game this weekend, so it was out of the question for her to go with me. She was upset, but what I like about her is that she does not nag and is not the argumentative type.

On the way to the airport Thursday morning, I told Meeka to look for me a condo. I felt like time was winding down before something jumped off and I needed to start making a move. I know Meeka has good taste, so she could narrow the choices down for me to a couple and I could look at them mid-week upon my return. I was going to be really busy when I got back, but I would check them out as quickly as possible. I gave her the specifics on what I wanted and the price range. Without saying I was leaving Diane, I believe baby girl got the idea and seemed very content on the direction things were going in. I gave her a passionate kiss at her gate. After a repeat performance this morning, I was hoping I would be able to hold out and concentrate at the tables this weekend.

Chapter Twelve

Meeka

I am so nervous going to this engagement party. I have not seen Michael all week. He spent a few more days than planned in Vegas and he just got back on yesterday. I was disappointed that he extended his stay in Vegas. At least he was able to stop by and see the condo's I had viewed. I really did not understand why he needed to be in Vegas all week, but I did not want to argue. We did not get to talk that much because during the day I had classes and at night he was at the tables. Being here, after not seeing him all week, definitely does not make it easier. All I want to do is be in his arms. I just don't feel good about any of this.

The one thing I do feel good about is how I look. I've never bought a dress for a thousand dollars, but I wanted to look fabulous tonight. If nothing else, I would work Michael's nerves. I did one of Nikki's numbers, black, with the back out, cut front down to my navel and the highest heels I could stand in. It was definitely sexy, but chic. The world of shopping has opened up to me and I'm starting to get good at it. Michael likes for me to look a certain way and to be able to meet his expectations, I've had to increase my mall attendance. I'm normally a jeans and tank top kind of girl. I could wear sandals or flip flops all year round if frost bite was not an obstacle in the cooler months.

I've been to other functions at this hotel and specifically in this ballroom. It's the smallest of all the ballrooms the hotel rents out. It's one of those that regardless of where you are in the room, you can see the other attendees quite well. So, it was not large enough to get lost in and that's what I wanted to do. I figured I would go in, mingle some and try to hang with some of my long-lost relatives. I know Diane and my mother would be together. I would not dare try to spend time with my mom tonight. Her radar would certainly be up with my dress and earrings anyway. The party started an 8:00pm and it was going on 9:00pm now. I was not trying to be that late, but Nikki bailed out on me when her latest conquest wanted her to go somewhere else. As she put it, "I can't pass up good loving for a chick fight". Which was low down, I had no plans on fighting Diane over Michael.

When I walk in, I see Michael standing to the left with some other guys. Hmmm odd. He has his wedding band on. Michael has never been one to wear his wedding ring even before we started seeing each other. My mother had mentioned that he had convinced Diane that with his work rings bothered his fingers, so he preferred not to wear them. The sight of him with it on now sent a cold chill up my spine. I did not make eye contact with him as I heard my name being called in the other direction.

My mother is waving at me from her table.

Of course, my father is right by her side and Diane is sitting there as well. I would guess the empty seat by Diane is Michael's. My dad gets up and gives me a hug and kiss. He pulls over another chair to their table. I hope they don't think I am going to sit here with them. I am getting sick to my stomach at this very moment. I lean over and give my mother a hug and kiss on the cheek. I'm really feeling annoyed at this point, especially after seeing Michael with that ring on. My mother comments on my dress. She mentions it must have cost a fortune. I tell her some lie, I can't remember now; but it shuts her the hell up. Diane is grinning ear to ear and definitely does not look like a wife in distress, or a wife whose husband is seeing me.

She is motioning for me to give her a hug and I have an out of body experience. I'm standing beside her as I see my body lean over and hug her. She mentions she has missed seeing me and I see my lips saying something. I don't do drugs so I know this can't be real. I sit down in the chair my dad pulled up.

I'm explaining to my parents that I have been so busy studying and preparing for finals that I have not thought anything about my upcoming twenty first birthday. I'll let them know what I would like to do when I give it some thought. Michael had already mentioned taking me to Jamaica or the Bahamas. Somewhere it is warm in November. My mom says she knows that maintaining a 4.0 GPA has to be tiring and that is why she understands that I have not been around as much. Then Diane says, she understands about being tired, she hopes that she is able to make it through the evening as she still has jet lag from flying in from Vegas.

I'm not a drama queen, but I swear when I stood up, I had to be the color of the white on a "skunk." I knew that if I did not get away from that table I would throw up all over the place. My mother asked what was wrong and I told her that I would be right back I needed to run to the ladies room. She stood up to go with me and I motioned for her to stay put I would be fine. I just had some Mexican earlier that has not agreed with me all day. I ran out of the ballroom and I'm not sure at what point I started crying. I passed the restrooms and ran straight out the entrance. I've never felt so hurt, disgusted and distraught at one time. The tears were streaming down my face. I was trying to wipe my eyes and find my car keys at the same time. Stuff started falling out of my purse. My hair was sticking to my wet face and I was trying to take deep breaths so that I would not throw up.

Michael comes up behind me. "Meeka, what the hell is going on." For some reason it took me a minute to realize who he was. Again, I'm not a drama queen; but I stood there behind tears and hair trying to figure out who is this man?

"Meeka, are you alright?"

"Don't you dare touch me!" I must have said it pretty loud because Michael had this I will slap the shit out of you look on his face. "I can't believe that you used me the way that you have. What sick type of man would do something like this? I trusted you Michael."

Michael pulled me into a nook right by the entrance. "What the hell are you talking about?"

"I'm talking about the freaking wedding ring on your finger. I'm talking about you taking your wife to Vegas."

"Meeka you need to calm down! Listen, before I left for Vegas, my cellular company called me on my phone to confirm where I wanted my call detail faxed to. I advised them that my call detail is and always has been suppressed. The guy told me yes, but I had requested to have the last three months worth of call detail faxed to me. He told me he was having problems with the fax number and needed to confirm with me. I asked him to read off the number he was trying to fax to and the number was to my home office with one digit off, which meant Diane had gone private investigator on me.

Whose number do you think she would have found on every day of the week?

I figured I needed to chill her out and try to make her feel like I wanted to work things out. I told her I wanted to work on our marriage, and I asked her to go to Vegas with me. I put the wedding ring on, so that she would really think I was sincere. Hopefully, once I move out, she will think I really tried and things just did not work out. At that point, maybe we can work through an amicable divorce without her trying to find or blame another woman for our breakup."

I know Diane.

No matter what happens she will always blame someone else for our marriage breaking up. She is the window bustin, car scratchin type that won't stop until her revenge is satisfied. If she would be honest with herself, she would know that it's really not about her not being a good woman, or any other woman for that matter, it's about us never being right for each other and me not in love with her. But she will go down fighting before she would ever submit to that reality.

I'm not sure if it's healthy to change emotions as radically as I did, but now I felt stupid. "Michael, why didn't you tell me you took her to Vegas?"

"Why would I, so you could sit back here with your imagination running wild? Meeka we are in a very delicate situation here baby, I need you to think. Why would I put down five thousand dollars of earnest money on a condo and set a closing date, if I was going to stay with Diane? I know you are young baby girl, but I need you to think more maturely. You come running up out of this motherfucka like you are in the Special Olympics. That does not help anything."

I could not help but to laugh, but understood what Michael was saying. I love him so much that I just lost it. He leaned over and kissed me. He asked me would he be able to have me tonight. I told him that he did not have to ask for what was already his.

He told me to go into the ladies room and wash my face and straighten up. As he watched me walking back in, he told me I looked really good to him. Neither of us knew that someone else had been watching us as well.

The remaining of the evening went well. When I returned to the party, I assured my parents I felt better and went and socialized with Deena and her family. When Deena introduced me to Todd, I knew that my cover would be blown; I was so nervous. I was waiting for Todd to say, oh, we met before, remember at the bar where Michael picked you up, but Michael was right; Todd acted like he had just met me for the first time. I think he picked up on how nervous I was. He asked Deena if it was okay to dance with me, so he could confirm my dancing abilities. He did not want me to mess up their wedding. We all laughed as Todd guided me to the dance floor.

It was a nice little upbeat song playing, so Deena did not mind me dancing with her man. Plus, I am her cousin. Todd told me that I looked like I was about to faint while Deena was introducing us. He did not want Deena to pick up on the fact that he already knew me. I was panicking and stammering so much, she may have thought we had messed around. I laughed and told him I was a neophyte mistress. We both fell out laughing. I saw Michael glance over at us with a questioning look on his face, which made us laugh even harder. By the time Diane dragged Michael onto the dance floor, I had made my rounds and could leave freely without seeming rude.

I could not bear to see Michael with her in his arms.

I'm not sure how he got away, but I met him after the party at the Hilton downtown. I did not realize how much I had missed him until he pulled me into his arms. We made passionate love and I hated to let him go. Whenever I'm away from Michael I just don't feel totally complete. It's hard to explain, but he has become such a part of me.

I have a doctor's appointment next week to start on birth control pills. When I mentioned to Michael that I was hesitant to go on the pill because I am a dancer and did not want to gain weight, he made no compromise about using a condom, only a snide comment that I would be gaining more weight than being on the pill if I did not do something.

He said he could not stay out late or that would defeat the purpose of what he was trying to do. I did not have a desire to stay in the room without him, so we left a little after midnight. It still pained me to see him putting his wedding band on as he walked me to the car. He told me he loved me and would call me tomorrow, but for some reason I was no longer feeling as secure in our relationship. That's probably the nature of being involved with someone who is married…..lack of security.

My mother had convinced me to come by on Sunday after church for dinner. It was really nice just sitting around the two of them like old times. I love both my parents very much. However, it has always been a special bond between my father and me. As far as I can remember, I have always been my daddy's little girl. I could not help but to imagine what my father would think and feel about me once he knew I was involved with Michael. Although he was not the one that spoke as harsh about Michael, like my mother did, I knew he did not care much for him either. We watched a little football and ate some dessert before I had to leave. When my mother walked me to the door, she made a comment that was odd. She asked me was I happy and I told her yes. She said that the happiness that we feel can sometimes be misleading.

She wanted me to stay focused and always be true to myself.

Chapter Thirteen

Meeka

Today I'm officially 21. It's hard to believe that I will be a legal wine drinker and be able to put up my fake ID. Nikki and I decided to go out tonight clubbing. It's been a while since we've been able to hang out together one on one. Michael did not sound really pleased about the idea, but since he was playing cards tonight, I don't think he could say much.

He, or shall I say we are supposed to close on the condo next week. Michael said he needed to make some additional cash to float on for the closing in order to put fifty thousand dollars down without using money Diane knew about. I'm not sure exactly how we were doing this, but I felt a little comfortable David was giving his legal advice. The deed goes in my name since this is a common law state and anything that Michael owns technically could be Diane's during a divorce. The mortgage however goes in Michael's name, since I have never worked a day in my life and Mr. Johnson says I will not in the future. However, it's a little strange having my name attached to a $500,000 piece of property that I could not pay for it if I wanted to. Michael was working it out with the builder on getting the cash down payment calculated in without tax issues. All I have to do is show up and sign on the dotted line.

We decided to put on hold the discussion about our living arrangements for now. I love Michael and I know we are sexually involved, but I never intended on living together without being married. When he mentioned he hoped the finalization of the divorce coincided with my graduation next May so I could move in, it surprised me. Anyway, that should be a very interesting discussion.

"Girl, I know you want to look better than me, since it's your birthday; but, sorry your little skinny butt will have to play second to all this." Nikki did look cute in her short skirt and thigh high boots. However, I do think I have her beat with my tight jeans on, suede halter and chocolate boots. We were good to go when my baby called and wanted to know where I would be just in case he finished up early. I told him which club I would be at, and I hope I could see him before my birthday passes.

Nikki and I hooked up with two other girls from the squad and made our way out. The good thing about hanging with other majorettes or sorority sisters is that you look cuter on the dance floor setting off your routines. The club we were going to was really nice. The crowd was mixed but did not have the thug types. It was more frequented by the 25-40 year old crowd, with a few outliers like my girls and me. I was having a blast and everyone who knows me, knows that I love to dance.

I had downed about two glasses of wine and was on my third when Jay comes up and wishes me a happy birthday. I told him thanks and tried to step around him. He blocked my departure and asked for five minutes of my time. I'm not a rude person and was kind of interested in what else was left to be said. He started talking about how much he missed me and that he was a real jerk for what he had done during our relationship. He wishes that there was something he could do to right the wrong and mend things. He also mentioned that he had seen me with my new man and wanted to confirm if it was as serious as it looks. I ask him, "How does it look?" He said he could tell that dude was evidently very familiar with my body by the way he carried himself with me. He finally got to the point he wanted to ask, had I lost my virginity to him? Because he was so sincere in his question and I really did not want to hurt his feelings even if he had hurt mine, I thought about a response that would let him know that he would never be in the running for me again.

Before I could say anything, I felt something cold on my back. I turned around and Michael was standing there looking as sexy as ever with a Heineken in his hand. Michael had on all black and it set his hazel eyes off. I quickly introduced Michael and Jay and turned my back towards Jay so that he knew our conversation had ended. Michael leaned over and gave me a nice kiss on the cheek and asked me to follow him so we could talk. We moved over to the corner of the bar where the noise was not as prominent.

"Baby, I'm glad you could make it."

"Are you sure?"

"Michael, of course I wanted you here. It's my birthday." He had this look on his face I had not seen before, and I was not certain what he was thinking.

"Meeka, don't let me come into a club or anywhere else for that matter and see you holding a conversation of any length with another man."

I really did not know what to say. I was startled that Michael was speaking to me like that. I tried to explain to him that Jay was casually talking to me and there was nothing to the conversation. Either he did not hear me, or he did not care.

"Meeka, all I need you to do is acknowledge that you heard and understood what I just said. I don't like repeating myself unless you did not hear me, damnit."

"Yes Michael, I heard you."

"Good, I don't think I ask for much. I just need you to do what I tell you to do."

He stood there looking at me like I was supposed to say something. So, I just mumbled, "Ok."

Michael led me out to the dance floor and whispered happy birthday in my ear. He said he had something very special for me later. As he held me in his arms, I was still in shock from our conversation, and he was acting like nothing unusual was just said. He gently kissed me on my lips, and I returned my tongue to him. The odd feeling dissipated as my love for him replaced it. He told me that he swept the table really quickly and that was why he was able to make it out tonight in time.

Since I knew there was a possibility that Michael would be able to meet me at the club, I rode with Nikki. Michael wanted to give me my birthday gift but said he would not be able to stay the night with me. I was crushed. Here it is a very important night, and my man could not even be with me. I guess all of those "other woman" articles I've read are really true. I told Nikki to wait on me at her car and I walked with Michael to his car. The club was still packed and so was the parking lot. I did not see Michael's car, but we were walking towards a black Lexus 470 SUV. Michael pulled out the keys and handed them to me. I must have had this dumbfounded look on my face, so Michael pointed the keys toward the SUV and unlocked the doors.

He leaned over and kissed me and told me happy birthday.

I started screaming so loud that Nikki and the other girls must have thought something was wrong. They came running over ready to beat somebody down. Tears were streaming down my face and I was trying to take deep breaths. I was holding Michael's neck and jumping up and down.

"What the hell is going on over here?" Nikki was looking straight at Michael.

"Michael gave me this Lexus SUV for my birthday!" All my girls started screaming and running around the car. I got in the driver's seat and

Nikki got on the passenger side. You would have thought I was 12 instead of 21. Michael was standing by the driver side window enjoying my pleasure. I leaned out the window and gave him the most sensuous kiss I could muster up.

He tasted so good and I wanted him so much.

I told him that it was too bad he could not spend the night with me, so I could show him how much I appreciated my new car. He told me there was no other place he would rather be, but he had to be smart during this time.

Michael told me to meet him at the dealership first thing in the morning, so I could sign the paperwork for the car title to be put in my name. I was joking with him, but I said, "Oh, a big car for a big family."

His smile faded and he said, "No, a big car for my golf clubs and more space for the trips we will take together."

I'm not sure if my heart sank because I knew this was going to be a huge hurdle that we would somehow have to overcome if we were going to have a life together, or if it was because I was already a week late.

Chapter Fourteen

Meeka

The energy around Homecoming is an experience to be remembered. Ours was even moreso because it was late in the year compared to other schools. We had a dance routine that was very complex, but all the girls had it down. The new outfits were in and they looked better than I expected. I actually was one of the few who voted no go for these outfits. They were too revealing for my taste and looked a bit hoochie. Nikki and I almost fell out. We'd had spats before, but she felt like I should have been taking her side in the voting. I have the body for it, but a sequenced halter and shorts with overly decorated thigh high boots just did not do it for me. Our routine called for a lot of bending towards the audience. Showing my bootie cheeks in the dead of winter or any other time was not sophisticated. If it had not been for me spending so much time out of the dorm trying to decorate the condo, I think we would have ended our friendship.

The band was so hot tonight.

I could not wait to hit the field. Every single routine we did in the stands was on time and in sequence. We stayed wrapped in our capes the entire time and the audience was anticipating what we had on. It was not as cold as I thought it was going to be, but just in case I had my mother hold some additional outerwear for me. I knew exactly where she was sitting because I was able to get some good seats. I only looked that way a couple of times and tonight I did not let Diane sitting with Michael get in my head.

Dancing is just as mental as it is physical, so I had to stay in the right mindset to do my thing tonight. I could feel the drums in my heart and the horns were sending tingles up my spine. The fact that we were winning going into halftime added another level of excitement and anticipation to the atmosphere.

As I led the squad down to the field, doing our exaggerated strut, I felt powerful and beautiful. Not because of any superficial reason of being cute or sexy or anything, but because we were ready to do what we came to do and that was perform.

As long as I can remember, even as a little girl, I was put out front. In private school the teachers seemed to be overly nice to me to prove that they were not doing things based on race. So, in play's I was Cinderella or Mrs. Claus. I was good at dancing, so in our performing lineups I was always in the center or the point in the V arrangements in my ballet and tap classes. But the highlight of attention always came from my dad. He made sure that I was picked up from school on time. He told my mother that he never wanted his little princess sitting around waiting to be picked up. When I would go to the mall shopping with my mother and there was something I wanted that she did not feel like I needed or deserved, as soon as I got home I would tell my father. He would practically demand that my mother tell him what store it was in and would take me himself to go back and get it. I don't think I'm spoiled from my experiences. I never have stayed out late, did drugs or participated in any questionable activities. I think being out front and supported by my father is what gives me the confidence that I now have to stand in the presence of forty thousand people and not be nervous not one bit.

We're on the last leg of our routine. The band is hopping, and I am sweating with a smile. On the last turn, we have to pause and pop. I see Nikki and she is beaming. I am the last one to drop into a split and the crowd goes wild! The way we are sweating you would never know its winter. We quickly put on our capes and dried off with our towels. I have to lead the squad out to the restroom and the concession stand to get something cool to drink. We are chatting like high school girls and the other students are gleaming with pride over our performance.

I see Michael coming towards me and I am smiling ear to ear, but he looks pissed. I'm not sure where my parents or Diane are so I don't try to hug or kiss him. He tells me to follow him, and we walk around the corner from the concession stand.

"Meeka, do you think what you have on is appropriate?"

"Michael, I don't pick out……" He would not let me finish my response.

"That's not what I asked you. Answer my question, Meeka."

My eyes started watering up as I knew I would not have a response that would satisfactorily answer his question. I could tell he was so angry at me. It seems like the last month or so, Michael has been quick to raise his voice with me. I find it intimidating and frightening. I think it's because of work, the condo, and the stress of knowing what we have to face when he leaves Diane.

"Baby, I did not want these outfits, but I was out voted."

"Out voted. You are a grown woman. You don't do what other people are doing based on some damn votes. Well, I hope you enjoyed having your ass out tonight, because this dancing mess is over."

"Michael, that's not fair. You know……"

"Meeka, did I just ask for your vote? Hell no!"

Just then my coach came over and told me it was time to go back in the stands. I told her I would be right there. She mentioned that we have to line up together to walk back in. I cannot believe that my man just told my coach that instead of worrying about a line, she needs to worry about living her fat ass dreams through how she is exploiting us in these outfits. She was too stunned to respond and just walked away. Michael told me he would call me tonight and that he was through talking about this majorette crap. He also walked away.

On the ride back to the dorm, I was so upset that I could barely see through my tears. I sat in the back of the bus, and everyone kept asking me what was wrong. I would not dare share my personal business with anyone and Nikki's hot butt did not follow the rules and ride the bus back with the rest of the band. I felt like a very important part of who I was had been ripped away. How could Michael make such a decision without considering my feelings or my opinion? I could understand some of his concerns and I was willing to hear them out, but he was not open to communicating with me. Conceptually, I knew that the love I have for Michael and the commitment I was making with him was much more important than being a majorette. I'm not that shallow, but the way things were playing out did not seem fair.

I know that some people think I'm passive.

My mom and Nikki especially are always telling me how I should be more vocal in situations of conflict. Nikki is always saying if we were not best friends, my butt would have been kicked all over the yard by now. Girls don't try me, because she is by me. I'm more than capable of speaking up for myself, but I don't want to debate about everything. Some things that would be a point of debate for my mom or Nikki, even as women, is not worth it to me. I don't think I need to prove myself to others. If that's passive, I guess I am then.

Nikki was in the room with what's his name when I got there. She was changing for their night out. I could tell she was still excited about the great performance we did. When I walked in, my face with the dried-up tears and streaked massacre were evidence of how distraught I was. Nikki stopped getting dressed and asked, "What the hell is wrong with you girl?"

"I can't talk about it right now, it's personal." Nikki asked her beau to step outside for a minute. He seemed annoyed and hesitated until she told him she would be right out.

"Meeka, what's going on?" I tried to open my mouth to explain, but all I could say, as I burst out in tears, was that the furniture was being delivered next week. I believe Nikki thought I had taken something to celebrate tonight and lost my mind. I was really trying to let her know how wrapped up emotionally, sexually, and financially I was in Michael that I had lost, no, I never had any control over anything in our relationship. I loved him so deeply that I knew my heart would break in two without him. I could never allow another man to make love to me and touch me the way he does. And now with the condo and the car, even if I wanted to exert some power, I could not because the furniture was being delivered next week and that was further evidence of how financially dependent I am on Michael Johnson because he needed to pay for it.

"Michael said I have to quit the majorette squad."

"Who the hell is he, trying to tell somebody what they have to do?" The last time I checked, your damn daddy's name was Mack not Michael. He has some nerve to upset you like this. I hope you told him where he could go straight to Meeka?"

"Nikki, you know how Michael is, he is so stubborn and set in his ways that I don't have a chance in changing his mind. He was so angry about the outfits we had on that I know he is dead serious."

"Angry, he is jealous. Meeka you have created a monster. And there's only one way to deal with the green-eyed monster. Let him think that you have walked. He will either change his ways or kill himself. Either way, you win."

As we were talking, I changed into my sweat suit and crawled into bed. I don't know if it was from all the crying or the hole in my heart; but I was not feeling well at all. Nikki looked at me and said I had turned completely white. My stomach was cramping something awful so I told Nikki that I needed to lie down. She gave me two Tylenol and I lay on my bed crying. I heard her at the door telling her friend that she was going to stay in tonight because she wanted to keep an eye on me. I was thinking I need to tell Nikki how much I love her and value her friendship as I fell off to sleep.

Chapter Fifteen

MICHAEL

The last place I wanted to be was driving to meet Mack and Linda for dinner. I cannot believe I can't think of a lie to tell Diane to get out of this. After seeing Meeka at the game, my tolerance level was at zero. I didn't want to make small talk with anyone, especially her parents and Diane. Diane was talking ninety miles a minute about the game, halftime, dinner and everything else. I was thinking the whole time how it would be nice to pull over and kick her out of the damn car. Meeka had really messed my head up tonight. If not for restraint, I could have gone out on that field and dragged her off.

When we got to the restaurant Mack and Linda were already seated. We did the normal greeting and Diane and Linda started chattering like birds. Mack tossed some small talk my way and I returned the favor. I really needed to talk with Meeka. I know she was upset, but so was I. I did not plan to be that harsh with her, but when I saw her I just exploded. This jealousness has got me crazy. I can't recall ever being this wrapped up in a woman. I love that girl too much.

Mack's cell phone rang. When I realized it was Nikki, it caught my complete attention. Whatever it was she told him caused him to abruptly push away from the table. We'll be there in fifteen minutes. He told Linda they had to leave because Meeka was not feeling well and needed to be taken to the hospital. He explained he was not quite sure what was wrong, but that Meeka was having bad stomach pains and could not walk or stand up straight. I asked what hospital he was taking her to and he said Saint Marks. Diane insisted that we go, but I told her to let Mack and Linda take her to the hospital first.

They said they would call as soon as they heard something.

I told Diane we should head to the house. I did 100 mph trying to get Diane home. I could not think fast enough on what I should do. I know I needed to keep my head and not do anything crazy, but I had to see what was going on with Meeka.

My cell phone rang. I did not recognize the number, but I answered anyway. "Hello."

"Michael, this is Nikki."

"Yes." I wanted to start drilling her, but I knew Diane was listening like the FBI.

"I'm really not sure if I should be calling you, but I think you would want to know that Meeka is headed to the emergency room. Her parents just picked her up and they are going to Saint Marks."

"Man, what's wrong with the car?" I knew Nikki was street smart.

"Oh, you're not alone. Listen, I know Meeka has not told you this and she will probably kill me, but I think you really should know, and she probably needs you. She might be pregnant."

"What!!!" I could not say anything else. Diane looked over at me with a quizzical look on her face. "Look man, I'm on my way, don't do anything as it could blow on you."

At 6pm, it had been a long day already. I could not eat earlier I was so furious from the Homecoming game that afternoon. We had not ordered dinner and was contemplating if we should. I quickly told Diane that I needed to head out to pick David up. He was stranded and that his car was smoking badly. She asked couldn't he get someone else because we may need to go to the hospital. I told her it should not take that long, plus I'm sure Linda will call if it's something she needed to go to the hospital for. I'd appreciate it, since we did not get to order dinner if she would fix a hot meal, so I'll have something to eat when I got back. That should keep her busy from trying to run to the hospital. She agreed.

I pulled out of the driveway with every intent to get to Saint Marks in record time. I had no clue what I would say or do when I got there. The thought that Meeka might be pregnant kept churning in my head. I could not wrap my mind around that concept. I knew I had been totally out of control sexually with her. No matter how much self-control I had used in the past with women, I could not make myself wear some latex before making love to her. This was not good at all. On the other hand, the thought was not as repulsive as I had thought it could be. Loving Meeka the way I did, the thought of her having my baby inside of her was okay.

I guess every time I thought about being a father, I associated that with some woman being the mother of my child and that was the turnoff.

Being the youngest of three, I was pretty much spoiled from the jump. My brother and I did not become close until later in life mostly due to the age difference. My sister was the middle child and between her and my mother nurturing was overflowing into my childhood. It felt like I had two mothers. My sister did everything for me when my mother was not available. If I was hungry and my mother was out shopping, my sister would cook for me. If I was upset about something, my sister would make whatever was wrong right.

My sister and mother were very protective of me.

My dad was also very active, *thank God*, as I probably would have turned out to be soft if not, but it was more from the sports and guy talk kind of way.

Unfortunately, my sister ended up getting pregnant when she was fifteen. I was ten at the time. All that attention she was giving me was directed towards the baby. My mother and father had to support her and her child, so they too, to a certain degree refocused their attention on my nephew. Although I loved him, I also resented him for taking my place.

I think that is where I first developed my phobia of kids.

I did not want to have any because I regarded them as taking away instead of what most people see as bringing fulfillment to their lives.

Then there was Stephanie. My freshman year in college I played baseball. I was on a full scholarship. Stephanie was my girl and I guess she thought that I would be going professional.

I was really good.

She decided to get pregnant to secure her ticket into some money. Her parents were devout religious people and when they found out, they forced her to get an abortion—go figure. I was very happy and left her with a quickness. She was probably equally happy as I tore my ACL that season and my baseball career never seemed to recover. One thing, I never went hatless sexing women again and that whole ordeal made me look at women totally different. I regarded women as vultures trying to get as much as they could even if it meant ruining people's lives.

What I really like about Meeka is that I know for certain she is a sincere and loving woman. She has no hidden agenda. Her character and integrity are intact and have not been diluted by the experiences of the world. If anything, the thought of her being the mother of my children brings warmth to me.

By the time I approached the hospital, I can't believe I was okay with Meeka being pregnant. How this whole thing would play out was still unknown.

Chapter Sixteen

Meeka

When the doctor came into the emergency room, he began to ask me a series of questions. The pains were coming fast and furious, but he would not give me any medicine until he understood what we were dealing with. He asked me could I be pregnant? With my mother and father standing on either side of my hospital bed, I was very apprehensive about telling him the truth. I was in so much pain though, I did not want to prolong getting some relief. I told him yes. I felt the air leave the room. The doctor immediately ordered a pregnancy test and an ultrasound. I was more concerned about Michael's baby than my parent's reaction. I did notice that my father did not blink or move when I told the doctor I could be pregnant.

My mother covered her mouth as if she were shocked or even embarrassed.

Something about the smell of hospitals make me sick and oddly enough, sad. My dad was in the hospital once when I was in middle school. I remember the aide coming from the Office to get me. My mom had sent Diane to pick me up and take me to the hospital. She did not know what was going on but reassured me that my dad was going to be fine. I was so afraid. My imagination can easily get away from me. All I could think about was my dad dying and leaving me alone for the rest of my life. How would my life be without a father? Who would make sure all of the bills were paid? Who would fix everything that broke? My dad was my everything and the thought of losing him engulfed me with such sadness. As we walked down the corridor of the hospital to find his room, I slid my hand into Diane's. Her hand felt so warm and comforting. Needless to say, he had a kidney stone, but that smell stayed with me.

Once the technician completed the ultrasound, she advised that the doctor would be coming back in to discuss the results. When I pressed her for the diagnosis, she said the doctor would have to review and discuss with me. My heart was so heavy. Over the past couple weeks, at the same time praying for my cycle to start, I was also falling in love with the idea of carrying Michael's baby. I knew that he would probably be highly upset, but I also knew that he truly loved me and would be there for me and the baby. On several occasions, I wanted to tell him, but with everything going on I felt like it was too much to throw on top of everything else he had to deal with. If it was a false alarm, it would have been better not to have even brought it up. That way we would not have to have the difficult discussion about how opposite ends of the family making spectrum Michael and I were on.

The other night, I came so close to mentioning that I thought I was pregnant. We were hanging out at David's and Michael had his head lying on my lap while he was watching the game. I could feel the warmth of his face against my stomach and my heart ached to tell him that we may be having a child together. I don't know if I was scared to say it because giving voice to the concept may have made it a reality that I was not ready to accept, or that it would put our relationship to a test that we may not have passed. I did not tell Michael.

My mother had the nerve to ask me if I wanted her to call Jay. Without even looking at her, I shook my head no. She went even further to say that he had a right to know what was going on. If it was not for the pain and fear that I was feeling, I would have burst out laughing. I did not respond, and she did not push further.

I lay there waiting for Dr. Black to come and tell me the fate of my baby.

Chapter Seventeen

MICHAEL

My intent was to walk into Meeka's room and be casual about my visit. I was going to tell Mack and Linda that I had to run out to help a friend with car trouble. Since it was located near the hospital, I decided to check on Meeka to give Diane a firsthand update on how her goddaughter was doing. When I walked into the hospital room, Linda was standing over to the right near the sink. Mack was sitting in the chair to my left. Once I saw Meeka lying in that hospital bed and her eyes started to fill up when she saw me, forget casual. I went straight to her bedside and sat right next to her. I could fill her heart beating inside mine. I leaned over and gave her the most tender kiss I could. She placed her hands around my face and neck and returned her love to me. Once I released her lips, I kept my forehead against hers and spoke to her very softly. Not because of Mack and Linda being present, but because I was trying my best to choke down the tears that wanted to come out of me. I gently laid my hand against her stomach where I believed my baby was.

"Meeka, why didn't you tell me?" I could have sworn I heard a brick drop from underneath Linda's skirt.

"Michael, I did not want you to feel pressured or trapped."

"Trapped, there is no way I would have felt trapped sweetheart. I needed to know that you were carrying my child. I deserved to know."

"I'm so sorry, Michael."

"No, I'm sorry. I should have been much more careful." Meeka explained to me that the doctor had ordered an ultrasound, and she was waiting for the results. I asked her if she would be okay while I went out of the room to talk with Mack. She nervously said yes.

I asked Mack to step out into the hall with me and without a word he started towards the door. I glanced over at Linda and for the first time, she was speechless.

"Mack, I really don't know where to begin. I guess I should tell you that I love Meeka and that I'm going to do everything to protect her and take care of her." I was shocked as he did not say anything or interrupt me. "I know this is a very awkward situation and puts a lot of pressure on everyone involved." I figured I would stop explaining as I was starting to sound guilty even though I was.

"How could you allow yourself to mess up my daughter's life? All the women in the damn world and you have to go after your wife's goddaughter. What kind of man cannot control himself to the point he would destroy his wife and his friendships? I trusted you in my home with my family and this is what you do? You screw around with my only daughter and get her pregnant. Even if you are that type of piece-of-shit of a man, how can you be so irresponsible to get her pregnant? You have the audacity to say that you love Meeka and that you are going to protect her and take care of her, yeah, right! What you are going to do is stay the hell away from my daughter. I really should have confronted you when I saw you with Meeka outside of the engagement party, but I would have had to acknowledge that my daughter was playing a role in this adultery, and I just wasn't ready to admit to that."

I would have never guessed in a million years that Mack saw me with Meeka that night. Damn that just shows how I'm completely careless and reckless when it comes to her. I don't plan on doing this again with another woman. Ms. Brown is going to have to be the last woman for me. It also proved how much Mack adored Meeka. He could not bring himself to believe that his daughter could be involved with a married man, or more than that *me*.

"Mack, first of all, I have not been involved with Meeka for the last four years, so chasing after her in your home or anywhere else has not been happening. I did not go out seeking to screw Meeka. We just happened to run into each other coincidentally and things just played themselves out this way. Trust me, I have enough problems of my own, and trying to intentionally fall in love with my wife's goddaughter was not something that I would have done, but it has happened and I'm not going anywhere. I'm going to leave Diane. I just needed some time to try and make this, as impossible as it sounds, not as damaging to everyone involved."

I could tell I was not getting through to him and if I had been playing cards, I would have thrown my hand in on this one, but I had too much at stake.

"Look Mack, I did not ask you to step out here to talk to try and convince you of anything. At the end of the day, when I leave Diane, I'm going to be with Meeka. I'm not looking for your blessing, your approval or anything else. I do hope that you do not drive Meeka away. I know she cares for you and I'd hate for that father daughter relationship to be ended because she was put in a situation that she had to choose."

I know that was a cocky move, but I don't have a lot of time to be playing around with Mack. He needed to understand what was at stake and I was willing to bet all I had that Meeka would choose me. I believe it would have turned into a fist fight if the doctor had not come by to enter the room. I stepped back and let him walk into the room first.

Dr. Black was in his late sixties and fortunately enough was Meeka's regular gynecologist. Unlike his name, he was a Caucasian man, short with a gray beard and a little overweight. I liked his bedside manner though; he seemed very concerned about Meeka as a person and not just a patient.

I was glad Meeka had a familiar face to help her through this.

Dr. Black explained that fifty percent of women will experience a spontaneous abortion during their childbearing years. It has no reflection on the woman's activities or predictions on future pregnancies. As he explained that the ultrasound showed that the fetus had no heartbeat and that Meeka was miscarrying, she was crying. I sat on the bed next to her and held her in my arms. Oddly enough, I was torn up inside. In little over an hour, I had changed my mind about having kids, fallen in love with the baby inside of Meeka, and then lost the baby.

The nurse came in to take Meeka to perform a D&C, which is a procedure to remove the fetus from the womb. When I leaned over her bed to give her a kiss, I could not hold back the moisture that had built up in my eyes. As tears slid down my face, Meeka wiped them away. I'm not sure how she saw my tears through her own. I can't remember the last time I cried, but my heart was hurting for the baby we lost and for Meeka. She was so torn up. She asked me would I be here when she returned, and I told her that I would not be any other place.

Linda could not wait to start pointing that judgmental finger in my face once Meeka was out of the room. She was ranting and raving on how much of a dog I was, and that this was over the top—even for me. She told me how crushed Diane was going to be when she found out. I explained to Linda the same thing I told Mack out in the hall. I also explained that the damage could be minimized as there was no need to bring Meeka into this at all. I was going to ask Diane for a divorce and move out. While we were going through the divorce proceedings she did not have to know about my relationship with Meeka. I did not want Meeka to be drug through the legal system in anyway. I think that idea resonated with Mack, as his body language suggested agreement. Once the divorce is over, if an explanation is needed, we can let Diane know that Meeka and I got involved after we separated. At that point it really did not matter to me.

"Michael, you must be out of your mind if you think I am going to lie to my best friend to help your black ass." Mack interjected and told Linda he saw it as more help for our daughter than for me. As Linda spun around to face Mack, I thought this was going to give me a break from being the center target for a couple of minutes.

"Mack, Diane and I have been friends for years and this is going to devastate her."

"It's going to devastate her more if she knows our daughter is involved. Why not let the divorce play out and keep Meeka out of it?"

"Meeka is in it, Mack! Contrary to what you may want to believe, your precious daughter has done something irreprehensible. There are consequences to actions and getting involved with a married man does have consequences, especially if you have no regard that it's your godmother's husband."

"Right about now, I don't give a damn about Diane or your friendship. All I care about is my daughter and what she is going through and as her mother that's what I would expect to be your first priority."

As Linda was burning a kryptonite hole into Mack, my cell phone rang, and it was Diane. I sent it straight to voice mail. Next, Linda's cell phone started ringing. She picked it up and glared at me. It was Diane and Linda explained to her that Meeka was out of the room having some more tests done. The doctor thought it was food poisoning and she should be just fine. I heard her end the conversation that there was no need to worry and she would speak with her tomorrow.

Chapter Eighteen

Meeka

My dad went out to bring the car around to take me home. I feel much better physically, but I'm still emotionally drained. My mother and Michael are following the nurse who is wheeling me to the exit. I'm not sure what happened while I was out of the room, but everyone has been rather quiet other than asking how I am doing. I can tell by Michael's eyes that quite a bit must have been said. Not only are Michael's eyes gorgeous, but they reveal every emotion that he feels.

He tries to be so tough, but his eyes give him away every time.

We have not been alone since I came back, so I'm in the dark right now. It was funny when the doctor told me I would be able to be released tonight and asked if someone could assist me in putting back on my clothes, both Michael and my mother reached for my things at the same time.

I guess Michael realized he was not going to win that battle.

He and my father stepped out of the room. My mother has not said anything and that is freaking me out. I know she must be upset and about to explode.

However, I am glad about going to my parents. It's truly my safe space. We moved into our current home when I was a junior in high school. My father is a Senior Vice President in Sales at a telecommunications company and my mother taught school until she decided that making a home was best for our family. I don't consider us rich, but we have a very nice four-bedroom two story home in the suburbs. I suddenly got a lot of friends when we built a pool.

I must admit my mom is the perfect homemaker.

Our home is modern and looks like it came straight out of a home décor magazine. More than anything though, my mom has always been there to make sure I was an excellent student. She took me to plays and put me in different educational camps. She wanted to make sure I was exposed to the arts and music. Even though she stopped teaching, she became my personal tutor.

As Michael is helping me get into the car, I was hoping that he would come to the house with me. I was surprised when my mother said he really should because we need to finish the discussion we started earlier.

Instead, he said he would try.

He had something he needed to take care of.

If it was not too late, he would come over, either way he would call me. In his eyes I saw a lot of pain. I wish there was something I could have done right there to make him feel better. I gave him a hug and a kiss and told him I'd talk with him later. It did not feel right to pull away with him standing there alone. So much had happened in this short period of time, I felt disconnected from Michael. It scared me that I did not know what he was feeling and thinking.

The car ride home was quiet.

I was kind of groggy, but I could sense there was tension between my mom and dad. I'm sure they were both disappointed and had a lot of questions to ask me. I don't think I've ever seen my parents have a real argument in front of me, unless it was about me. They have such a strong and loving marriage. I always hoped to find a man just like my dad. My dad probably won't admit it, but they are similar. Michael is very protective of me. I feel safe with him, and I know that he will take care of anything that comes up. He is also a provider like my dad. I sense this need to be responsible for the people he loves and to ensure that they are cared for.

My house was about a 35-minute drive from the hospital. By the time we got home, I was sound asleep. My mother gently nudged me to wake me up. The softness in her eyes was enough to help me exhale. Just maybe we could all get through this.

Chapter Nineteen

MICHAEL

On my way home, I realized that out of all the things I've ever had to do in my life up until this point, this was probably the most difficult. This has been a whirlwind of a day, and I did not know how to begin to handle the worse to come. It was about 8:30pm when I pulled up into the driveway. I thought about how much I had wanted Diane and me to sell this house and build another one. I agreed to stay here at her house after the marriage until Diamond finished high school in two years. After that, we were having so many problems that I did not push the moving issue and two more years had come and gone. When I opened the garage and saw Diane's car a sinking feeling sat in on me. I got out of the car and smelled fried chicken and biscuits. I had forgotten that I asked Diane to cook dinner before I left.

When I walked into the house Diane was reading the paper in the family room. She looked up and asked where I had been. I told her that we tried to work on the car to no avail. We then waited to have the tow truck pick it up. The time flew by. She said that she had gotten worried and called David's house. No one answered, so she left a message. After being friends for so long, David knows not to pick up the phone if his caller id shows my house number unless he is expecting me to call from home. He won't be calling back either.

I sat down in my chair and started flipping through the channels. Diane asked if I wanted her to fix me a plate. Although I was hungry, I did not think it would be right to eat and then tell her I was leaving her. This was causing me a lot of consternation than I thought. I really did not want to hurt this woman. Diane has never done anything to me, but try to love me. She has forgiven me repeatedly for my indiscretions. This was not fair, but it really was not fair to keep giving her false hopes about our marriage.

"Diane, we need to talk." She came and sat down on the couch closet to my chair.

"Ok, honey what's up?"

"You know over the last couple months we've been really trying to make things work." I had not rehearsed what I wanted to say because I was planning to speak from the heart. The truth was things have never been right and I did not think they ever would be.

"I know Michael. I have noticed that you are trying and that makes me feel so good. I love being your wife and I want our marriage to work out. When we first got together you changed my world. You made me a little crazy, but for the better."

"The problem is Diane I should not have to really try. I don't think that is how a marriage should be." She looked confused and moved to the edge of her seat. "I don't want to have to continuously try and make something work. I know a marriage is effort, but without the feelings it's not worth it to me. I mean I care about you and I want the best for you and Diamond, but I don't think that either of us is getting the best out of this relationship."

In retrospect, the trip to Vegas may not have been a good idea. I was doing it to deter Diane from finding out about Meeka, but I really gave her false hopes about our marriage. There was no other way, but I felt bad about leading her on the way I had, especially now. I'd been wearing my ring, coming home at decent hours and having sex with her more regularly. I may not be the best guy in the world, but I don't intentionally mislead and hurt people.

"Michael what are you saying. I love you and I am willing to spend the rest of my life trying to make us okay. Those are the vows I took when I married you."

"I'm not willing to do that. I'm saying that I'm calling it quits." Over the past several weeks I had been putting on my best acting, but you would have thought that we have had the perfect marriage over these four years and that I had never cheated on her or anything. She acted like this was catching her totally off guard.

"Michael, we are not divorcing. I am not going to give up on our marriage. We have not even gone to counseling. You need to be more specific o[n what] it is you need from me for me to change."

"Diane, I need you to really listen and he[ar me.] I am not in love with you. I do not want to be married to you any longer. You don't need to change you need a man that can love you for who you are."

"Who is she, Michael?"

This is exactly what I did not want to happen. I did not want Diane to go focusing on blaming someone else for our failed marriage. Granted I've screwed around, but the truth is if I really had feelings for her, we could make our marriage work. The desire for other women would not be an issue. The problem is between the two of us, not anyone else. I know she would never admit that.

"Listen, I'm going upstairs. I'm packing my stuff and I'm going to stay at David's until I get a place. I don't want this to be a long and drawn-out divorce. I know that you can provide for yourself. You had this house before you met me. If you need some support for a few months, I will definitely do that; but this marriage is over."

I started walking out of the room and she was crying. She was begging me to stay at the house. Even if we did get a divorce I might as well just live there until it is final. When she told me she would not live without me and was going to kill herself that really pissed me off. I know Diane and one thing I know is how strong she is. She would be just fine. I hate when anyone tries to manipulate me and I think she saw that saying that lie did not bring compassion from me, but only frustration. I walked away.

She got up and followed me upstairs. I really don't need this right now. She quickly moved to the next stage of grief, which I believe is anger. She started saying I had to be seeing some bitch again. I think the grass is going to be greener on the other side, but I am completely wrong.

What kind of man would walk out on his wife?

If I was a real man, then I would know how to make a marriage work.

I'm nothing but a little punk and she would not be surprised if David and I were on the down low.

When I realized I had put my hand around her neck and pushed her against the wall, I immediately regretted it. I'm not homophobic, but I hate someone challenging my manhood.

"Look Diane, don't do this, okay? I do not want this to turn into something ugly. You need to accept the fact that this is over. It's not about another woman or a man. It's about moving on."

After I had packed a few suits and casual clothes, while she was standing there staring a hole in my back, she moved into denial. I did not realize you moved through the grief stages so quickly. When she told me I would be back. I'd be begging her to take me back and she would just slam the door in my face I almost wanted to laugh, but it was so sad. She left the room and went back downstairs. I was trying to remember where I had put my gun. The last thing I needed was for her to go Texas Chainsaw up in here and I not be strapped. I remembered it was in the car. I had taken it with me when I went gambling last week. I had quite a bit of cash in the house and even though it was in my safe and Diane did not know the combination, I decided to put the money in my duffle and just get a new safe later.

When I went downstairs to start loading things in the back of my car, she was sitting at the kitchen table eating dinner like nothing had happened. That's when I decided to get the rest of my stuff later and get out. Women are strange creatures, and I did not want to take a chance of things negatively escalating.

I was not ready to deal with Meeka's parents after this ordeal with Diane, so I headed to the condo. I called David and told him what had gone down. I asked him to draw the papers up tomorrow and have her served. I did not want to prolong this one minute. He wanted to know was I *really* okay? I asked him was he gay and I started laughing. I was laughing so hard I was not sure when he hung up on me.

When I opened the garage door at the condo and saw Meeka's SUV in the garage a smile came over my face. At least baby girl can get some wear out of her car now, since she has been keeping it low key from her parents. Every time I walked into the condo, it amazed me how similar Meeka's and my taste were. Although it was taking forever to get some damn furniture, I knew she was picking out exactly what the place needed. Meeka is always telling me how frugal she is, but when it comes to decorating that girl was off the chain. A couple of times I had to say no. I don't know what a French Mahogany Retro Chair is, but for five grand for one chair it would not be here.

All thirty-five hundred square feet of the condo was hardwood. The kitchen was Meeka's favorite room. She had the builder put in marble kitchen counters, these nice cabinets with glass doors and an island stove that she promised she would be cooking on. But for tonight, I would be finding a cozy spot on these hard hardwood floors. At least the guy had come out and hung up my 85" inch flat screen. While I would be hurting on the floor, I could be enjoying ESPN and a nice fire. I went into the master bedroom because I remembered Meeka had all these bags of stuff in there. Finally, some luck my way tonight. I know Meeka is going to kill me, but this $800 California King comforter will make me a nice temporary bed on the floor.

When I called to check on Meeka she was doing well. She was hungry and so was I. I told her I would pick something up and bring it to her. She would have to give me a minute because I was going to eat my food at the place. The last thing I wanted to be doing was sitting around Linda eating. When Meeka was getting dressed to leave the hospital, Mack and I had agreed to give Meeka time to recover before we discussed the relationship further. I was okay with that. I'm not sure if he is thinking Meeka will have a change of heart, but I'm not worried about her loyalties. I'm a good judge of things and Meeka is mine.

I stopped off at our favorite little seafood place. I felt like some cognac before I ordered my food. I had downed three and started on my fourth one before I knew it. Since I had not eaten all day, this went straight to my head. I decided not to eat at all as I would have been sick as a dog. I ordered Meeka's seafood pasta and sat waiting. I heard a very familiar voice come up next to me.

"Hi, sweetie."

"It was Sherry and I have to admit she was looking delicious." Every bone in my body was telling me to get up and get the hell out of there, but I had not gotten Meeka's food yet.

"Can I sit down?"

I motioned for her to have a seat.

"No, can I sit on the side of the booth with you?" When I turned and looked up at her she was looking hot as hell. The top she had on was only showing cleavage and this woman had much body. I think her entire butt weighed more than Meeka. I started remembering how I used to enjoy riding it. I slid out of my seat to let her in. She rubbed up against me and I was instantly turned on. When I sat back down there was little to no small talk. She told me how she had been missing me and wanted to prove it to me. Before I knew it, she had grabbed my crotch and started massaging. I knew it would be a while before I could be with Meeka again and the thought of it made me vulnerable. I leaned over and kissed her on the neck and felt her breast.

I drug her to the men's restroom and balanced her inside one of the empty stalls. She had on a dress that provided me easy access to her play area. Damn, she did not have any panties on. I stuck my finger inside her and felt the wetness that I needed to penetrate. I patted my back pocket and remembered I had not carried a condom in months. I was not using them with Meeka and did not keep any on me.

"What's wrong baby, get him in me." I remembered how Sherry liked a good ride.

"Damn, Sherry I don't have a condom. Do you have one in your purse?"

"Michael, no; but you know I'm on the pill. It will be okay baby you're the last man that I've been with." I was drunk, but I remembered something my mother always said. "There's always an out in the time of temptation; most people just don't take it." Well, Michael Johnson is no fool and I had a lot at stake including losing Meeka and or dying. I dropped Sherry down and walked out.

When I got to Meeka's door, I had decided it was best not to go in because I was still intoxicated. I'm glad she answered the door. I apologized for how long it took me. Evidently, I was extremely late because she looked way past pissed. I could also tell that she must have been asleep.

"Michael, I can't believe you came over to my parent's house this late and drunk."

"Baby, I've been through a lot today and I know that I've had too much to drink, so I was not planning on coming in." She opened the door some more and looked me up and down.

"Not only are you drunk, but you've been with some whore! You've got red-ho-lipstick all around your shirt collar on both sides. I can't believe you would be out doing this after all I have just gone through. My parents were so right about your trifling tail. I lost our baby today and you are out screwing around. Michael, you need to leave and don't ever call me."

She was crying as she slammed the door in my face.

For some reason, I could not muster up a response fast enough. I did not dare knock on the door as I knew Mack or Linda would answer this time. I stumbled to my car thinking this must be what rock bottom feels like. At least I made it back to the condo.

Chapter Twenty

MEEKA

I'm so tired of crying. It seems like all I've done lately is cry over this man. How in the world could he do this to me? I've been through so much today and just needed him to support and comfort me and he goes out and is with some other woman. I am such an idiot.

I intentionally avoided my parents and headed straight to my room. The last thing I needed was I told you so, or Meeka you were just infatuated. I would just die if I had to listen to my mother. It was bad enough, Diane's crazy-self had called here screaming in the phone. My mother talked to her about an hour regarding Michael leaving her. I could not hear what Diane was saying, but from the comments I heard from my mother I could tell she was torn completely up. My mother offered to go over to her house and stay with her, but my father gave her *the hell if you will* look—she eloquently backed out of that offer. The good thing was my mother told her not to do anything stupid. She had seen on Divorce Court where the wife had burned all her husband's stuff and was held liable for it. Right about now, I wish she would burn Michael's crap completely up.

She told my mother that Michael was staying at David's house. I forgot that my mother and father did not know about the condo yet. I decided I had better not say anything. The less they knew the less they would have to try and keep from Diane.

My cell phone had been ringing off the hook. Michael had called ten times in one hour. I hoped he would eventually give it up. Unlike my breakup with Jay, this was much more devastating. My heart was so wrapped up in Michael that I could barely breathe thinking that it was over between us. How could I have been so stupid? Why did I think he was going to be different with me? I was not sure what I would do, if anything, about the house or the car. I'm sure Michael would pay for everything since he could keep both of them. I would demand that he puts the condo and SUV in his name after his divorce is final. I don't know if I had told him what day next week the furniture was scheduled to be delivered, or when the drapery company would be coming to hang the remaining window treatments, or when the guy was coming back to finish some work on the deck of the bedroom. *I hate him.*

As I lay in my bed, I practiced self-talk. I decided after this weekend I would get back to campus and bury myself in my studies. I can't believe it is almost the beginning of the New Year and I had not set any goals. I will be graduating in May and had not even begun to look for a job. I should have at least an intern opportunity lined up, but Michael did not want me to work, so I had listened to him. I also needed to start working on the routine I would perform for

Deena's wedding. I don't care if Michael is there or not, I will not let him have any more control over my life. I am also going to majorette practice. We only have a few more games and I don't care what Michael thinks. I'm crying again, but at least I did get some self-talk done.

In the morning, I'll convince my parents that I'm fine and go back to the dorm. I spoke to Nikki once I got out of the hospital. I'm so hurt by Michael I don't think I will even share this with Nikki. Enough, I need to get some rest my body has gone through so much.

My eyes get heavy, and I cry myself to sleep.

Chapter Twenty-One

MICHAEL

It's the middle of the week and Meeka has not called me back. Diane is bugging the hell out of me, and I guess I'm doing the same to Meeka. I left her messages that we really need to talk. I can't believe she would just turn her back on our relationship like this. I've got to make her understand how much I love her and that I can't live without her. I can't believe I was that stupid to get that close to Sherry. When it rains, it floods.

She could at least let me know what's going on with the furniture. I've been sleeping on the floor for four nights and my back is killing me. I don't have the company name, number, and I don't know the day and time of delivery. I tried to call her directly in her room, but she has conveniently not been there. I can tell Nikki is lying, but she's funny with her thug self, trying to be so hard when I call.

Todd even wanted to know if I was okay with Meeka dancing in their wedding once we discussed what had gone down. The wedding was weeks away and I was not planning on Meeka and I being split up that long, so I told him yes. Worst case, it would give me an opportunity to see her. I don't seem to be doing so well with that right now. I don't want to just go looking for Meeka because I don't know if Diane is stalking me. Once she got the divorce papers, she took crazy to a whole other level. She called my mother and my sister begging that they intervene to save our marriage. My folks don't even like Diane, especially my sister Tia. She felt like Diane was "old" and all wrong for me.

I wish I had listened to her.

Now my mother is all upset and was thinking about calling the family reunion off this weekend. I don't know why women are constantly linking one thing to another when there is no connection at all. What does my pending divorce have anything to do with our family reunion?

When I drove up to Meeka's dorm, I saw her car in the parking lot. I know that she does not have a class currently and is usually in her room or the library. I saw one of the girls that was with Meeka at her birthday celebration at the club. She gladly escorted me into the dorm, so I did not have to call Meeka's room only to get hung up on. I believe she said her name was Leslie. Leslie thought that Meeka was in her room because she had seen her earlier. I told her I was trying to surprise Meeka, so if she could knock on the door and let Meeka think it was her, I would appreciate it. Ms. Leslie obliged.

"Hi Meeka, its Leslie." The door opened and I saw my baby. She was looking a little thin and sad, but she was still gorgeous. Once she saw me, I know she wanted to slam the door, but it was obvious she had not told any of her girls other than Nikki that we were done. Leslie grinned and walked away. Before Meeka could close the door, I moved my body through the door frame. Good, Nikki was not there.

"Michael, please leave. I can't do this with you right now."

"Ok, when can you do this Meeka?" I wanted to grab her and show her how much I loved her right then and there, but I knew I had several weeks to go.

"I'm trying to get over you and move on with my life. I've never been so hurt and it's very difficult for me right now. I know we will have to talk about the condo and other outstanding items at some point, but I just can't do it right now." I could tell she was about to start crying.

"Baby girl, I'm not trying to get over you. I know I messed up big time, but baby I did not sleep with anyone. This past Saturday was like no other I've ever had. Everything that could have gone wrong did. The baby, your parents and Diane was a lot. I know I should not have drunk so much, but that seemed to be numbing me and I needed that. By the time I ran into Sherry, I was drunk. She was all over me and I won't lie Meeka I was vulnerable, but baby I swear I did not have sex with her." I decided to leave out the fact that I did not have a condom and that was probably the only thing that stopped me. Really and truly, I did not know. Even with a condom, the man upstairs may have given me another way out.

"Meeka, you know what we have is good baby and you know in your heart that I love you girl.

Please don't throw that all away because of one extreme night."

"Michael, how can I trust you? How do I know when you are put in a situation where you have to say no to being with a woman that you will?"

"Because I'll remember the expression on your face that made me ashamed of who I was. After all that you had gone through with the baby, I failed you. I'll think about the tears that you shed after I told you that I would never hurt you and then I turned around and I did. Meeka I'm not a perfect man. I've got a lot of shortcomings, but I can honestly say that I'm thirty years old and have never been in love until I met you. Baby I need you let's work this out." I really needed her to understand how I was feeling.

It's difficult for me to express my feelings and put my heart out on the line, but I can't imagine my life without her. Within less than six months this girl has changed my entire world. I've learned more about love and commitment than I ever even knew existed. If I needed to spend the rest of my life trying to get Meeka to forgive me at least I had some long-term goals. I would be damned if another man would enjoy what is mine.

When she walked into my arms, I made myself a pact. That if I ever cheat on this woman, I will let her go myself. I won't drag her through any changes. I won't be the selfish man I've been, trying to have it all. "Baby, I've been so worried about you. I know losing the baby and then our fight was a lot to handle in a single night. I feel so bad about not being there for you like I should have. I plan to make all this up to you." I kissed her sweet lips and I know it had to be several minutes before I pulled away from her and asked her, "When can I stop sleeping on the floor?" She laughed and told me the furniture would be delivered on tomorrow.

The furniture was in, and my baby and I were back in stride again. I needed to make an appearance at the family reunion, and I would head straight back home to be with Meeka.

Back home to be with Meeka.

I liked the sound of that.

Meeka and I have not broached the subject of her moving in yet, but we need to discuss that real soon. This back-and-forth condo/dorm thing was not what I wanted. I did not want to push too much because I stayed firm on quitting the majorette squad. She really did not fight me as much as I thought she would. I overheard her telling Nikki, that even though Dr. Black said there is nothing she did to lose the baby she did not think dancing so hard could have helped.

Meeka and I both agreed that it would probably not be a good idea for her to meet my family yet since the divorce was not final, or I was not sure where Diane's head was. Two days had gone by, and psycho had not called. I am hoping she is on the last phase of grief, *acceptance*. I have my fingers crossed because I really want to move on with my life. I did not know how exhausting this whole ordeal would be on me and Meeka.

I did not realize that I had not spent a lot of time with my folks lately. Between trying to see Meeka and keep Diane at bay, my time had been occupied over the last few months. My sister told me that my mother seeing me was a relief. She had been very worried about me. Pops was cool as always. I was able to still away and share some of my life's detail with Tia. I told her about Meeka and how much I cared for her. Tia was in awe. She could not believe I was even using words like care and love. She said that's how she knew Diane was all wrong for me. Even when I told her about asking Diane to marry me, she said I never once used the word love. Funny how other people can pick up on something like that and you are so in left field.

Tia knows me better than any woman. She asked me how I was managing my temper. I've always had this little thing with my temper that either kept me in trouble or kept me on the verge of getting in trouble. Tia was always there to help bail me out. She literally had to bail me out of jail once over my temper. She knows first-hand how easily I can be set off. I'm very protective of my family and especially Tia. She was dealing with this guy who made the mistake of smacking my sister. When I hopped out of my car in front of his apartment, all I saw was red. No one could pull me off of him until he was almost unconscious. One of Tia's friends called her and told her I had been arrested. She of course called David and they had me out in a few hours. Jail is no place for me. It's good to have friends who have friends. The incident did not make it to my record. The bad thing about that incident is that my sister does not tell me much. Sometimes I feel like my family, except my dad, walk around on eggshells with me.

With Diane, my temper flare-ups were usually provoked. An incident happened very early in the marriage when Diane was still used to being independent. She had this habit of doing what she wanted to do, even after I would tell her to do something differently. I have this pet peeve about my wife being home when I get there from work. Diane went in very early and was off in plenty of time to be home. After I had mentioned it to her on a couple of occasions, she still decided to do things her own way.

One evening I got home, and she was not there.

I did not call her, and she did not call to check in.

A couple of hours later she came home with some shopping bags and acted as if we had never discussed her being at home when I got there. I had had a few beers and when I asked her why she did not come straight home, she got all diva on me and told me I was trying to control her and what she did.

She started running off at the mouth about being a grown woman. The finger wagging started, and I snapped.

Diane has always been good about running her mouth, but I think she understood after that night that things had changed.

Diamond got scared and called the cops—they took me downtown.

Again, Tia came to the rescue. She came down and bailed me out and since Diane never pressed charges or gave a statement and Diamond only heard us scuffling and did not see anything, there were no charges filed.

I told Tia that I'm cool and I think a lot of my issues must be with being matched with personalities that conflict with mine. *It's a lot different with Meeka.* Although Meeka is very intelligent, she is not boxed into this independent thinking and she's not argumentative. She wants to please me, and I want to please her, so we don't have a power struggle going on in our relationship. Tia gave me her traditional big sister speech on me keeping a cool head and then she started in on if I was still gambling. Funny how she always wants me to break bad habits, but she's the first one in line when she needs me to break her off some cash. I have no problems taking care of my sis when she's in a tight spot though.

Her husband is cool but does not make enough to always make ends meet. If he's okay with the help, I don't mind.

At the end of the reunion, my mother mentioned that she and Tia will be at Todd's wedding. They got their invitation and love March weddings. It should be a nice wedding with my three special ladies around.

Chapter Twenty-Two

MICHAEL

It's been two months since Diane was served with the divorce papers. David called and said that he spoke with her attorney, and she has agreed to the final revisions of the divorce decree. I agreed to pay alimony for a year. I really did not have a problem doing it even though Diane was only asking to be vindictive. I'm glad that I am careful with my gambling winnings and pay some amount of taxes, at least on the Vegas winnings. Diane's lawyer was digging big time to demonstrate that my income was a significant loss to Diane. Since we had not changed our lifestyle too much since the marriage and we did not have kids, she was fortunate to get a damn dime. Once we go to court and both sign the papers there's really nothing left.

A couple weeks afterwards, I will be a single man. Some of the guys wanted to throw me an "After Divorce" party. I did not think that would go to well with Meeka. Technically, I'm still committed just with someone I *want* to be committed to.

Meeka finally moved in the other day. I was at my breaking point on this back and forth to and from the dorm. She only has a couple of months left before she graduates, and she might as well make the move now. I need her in my bed every night and want to wake up to her every morning. I told her that I plan to marry her, but I just needed a little time after the divorce. She understood that and really thought that we should not live together during that time. I told her that there was no way in hell that I would be coming and going from her parent's house after she graduated and since I did not want her to work what did she think she would be doing at their house? She needs to be with me making a home for us. I think she is the perfect little homemaker and once she finishes school we can really settle into our life.

Her parent's still do not agree with us being together, but at least we are as cordial as can be. Linda finally agreed to keep Meeka and my relationship from Diane. She is convinced that this will eventually destroy their friendship. I hope it does not. Diane needs a friend and I hate to admit it, but Linda is as faithful as they come. Mack hates me, but he loves Meeka so much that we can tolerate each other. We don't hang out or anything, but when speaking is required, we exchange pleasantries. All hell broke loose when Meeka went to the house to pick up her clothes when she was moving. She kept the alternate season of clothing at home. I told her I wanted her to completely move in from the dorm and her parent's house. Linda called me and cursed me out about having her daughter live with me out of wedlock. I told her just like I told Meeka we would be getting married. Of course, that did not satisfy her or Mack, it made them madder. I've got to find a way to keep Linda out of this marriage. I know it will be harder since Meeka is her daughter and we will all be a family.

Man, if I did not love Meeka as much as I do, I would run in the opposite direction.

Meeka is getting frustrated keeping our relationship a secret, especially now that her parents know about us and she has officially moved in. The other night we were at one of my boy's place for a boxing fight. I was not trying to hide my relationship with Meeka, but I was not overly affectionate as I usually am. A lot of that had to do with this female that was a friend of Diane's being there. I knew she and Diane had been in contact and she would be running back to Diane telling her everything she saw. Meeka could tell I was being distant, and this really pissed her off. I can understand how she feels, but she knows what we are trying to do. The last thing I want is for Diane to start tripping if she knows I'm involved. Meeka did something that I did not expect. She was letting this guy give a little more attention than she knows I appreciate. I pulled her to the side and told her to chill with the conversation with that guy. She never has tried to push my buttons, but that night she was on the border. I'm not sure if she was that frustrated or the wine was making her a little cocky, but she had an attitude that I knew I needed to straighten out.

At the end of the night, we left, and I was boiling. I tried to explain to her that what she was doing at the fight is just how to get somebody killed. Women start a lot of stuff between men all because they are trying to prove a point. When I asked her what she was trying to prove, she wanted to know how long I expect to keep her as my secret "friend."

She felt like she has been giving a lot to the relationship and not getting much in return.

She wants a normal relationship where she can be with a man without worrying about who sees them together or where they go.

The other woman crap was getting old, and she did not know how long she could put up with it.

There were plenty of men out there that would be proud to have her openly on their arm.

I pulled the car over because I wanted to be clear and for her to understand where I was coming from. "Meeka, I don't know where all this mouth is coming from, but you need to chill with it. You know what I'm trying to do and how fast I'm trying to do it. If you think there's another guy out there that you need to be with, then go be with him. I don't have time for these little girl games."

I guess she got the message because the remainder of the ride was in silence.

One thing about Meeka, she is not the type to stay upset for long. She pouts some, but quickly recovers. She must have known she was wrong and how serious I was about not playing games. She fixed us a nice hot bath, lit some candles, and poured two glasses of red wine. After we exchanged massages, she made sweet love to me. It drives me wild when she is the aggressor. She's still learning, but she's mastered showing me how much she cares and wants to please me.

The next morning as I was leaving the house, seeing her lying in my bed with that sweet smile on her face made me count my blessings. I can't remember wanting to get home every day as quickly as possible.

Chapter Twenty-Three

Meeka

I'm at home today and I've got quite a bit to get done. I really like being here with Michael. It's funny because I remember playing house as a little girl, but I don't recall the man being there. I remember my kitchen set and cooking. I remember my babies, which were all the dolls I had; but I don't remember the baby's daddy. Funny how you omit certain things from your make-believe games as a child. I know this is not house, but making a home for Michael is something that I really love doing. I was not big on not working, but I have enough to do for now. Studying a couple of hours each day, keeping the house clean and making dinner keeps me pretty busy. Plus, I have been working on my dance routine in preparation for Deena's wedding in a few weeks.

Ever since I expressed my frustration to Michael on this whole incognito relationship, he has been trying to do everything he can to appease me. I would never leave Michael for anyone, but I'm just so worn from all of this.

At least there is light at the end of the tunnel. I talked to Michael earlier and the court date for the final decree is in three weeks. I am so glad this will finally be over, or this phase of all this will finally be over. I'm sure there is going to be more drama to come once Diane finds out about Michael and me. My mother constantly reminds me that we've yet to experience the devastation that we have caused. She is so dramatic.

Diane came over while I was moving. I had the Lexus SUV because it holds so much more. Nikki was with me, so I told Diane it was her car. I had to let her drive my car when we left, and Nikki was in full form. Diane asked me where I was taking my things and I told her that Nikki and I were getting an apartment together. My mother was right, once you start lying it's hard to stop.

At least it was only one person that I had to lie to.

She had the nerve to say that I could have moved in with her and had my own space. She was lonely in the house now that she and Michael had split. Although Diamond started college at the same time I did, she was behind on graduating by a full year.

I did not ask why but I could guess.

If Nikki is a borderline ho, Diamond was the mother of all ho's.

Diamond and I grew up together. She was born a few months before me and with our mother's being best friends, they had hoped the same for us. As little kids, we played well together and were very close. As we got older, we never just seemed to click. Although our mothers have similar interests, we did not. I think we also resented the forced friendship that our mother's put on us. Plus, because my dad and mother were married there were some things that I was able to have and experience that Diamond did not. Diane did well in providing for Diamond's needs, but my parents were able to afford much more for me. The ballet, tap, and gymnastics were too expensive for Diamond, so she did not have those exposures.

Diane scraped to send Diamond to private school, but after ninth grade she could not afford it, plus Diamond was not scholarly. We still saw each other during our high school years, but Diamond took a route that was not inviting to me. I believe she lost her virginity in tenth grade and eventually had an abortion. She had gotten pregnant by some guy in her neighborhood. I don't think to this day that Diane knows. I'm glad we lost touch as I don't know if I would have been able to be with Michael if Diamond and I were still friends. That would have meant breaking two people's hearts that I really cared about. I still find myself thinking about Diane and how kind she has been to me.

She is one of those people that took her godmother duties very seriously.

Every significant activity in my life she was always there. For my birthday, she would always get me a savings bond. I did not really appreciate them at the time, but once I started school, they were very helpful. For Christmas though, it was always toys and clothes. I remember for my high school graduation, she, Michael, and Diamond came. I hardly remember Michael, but I know he was there. I really do love Diane and wish there was some way to salvage our relationship once all of this comes out, but that is totally unrealistic.

I told Nikki to have her behind here by 4:00pm because I needed to run some errands before Michael got home from work. He wants me home when he gets here, plus I do not want him to know that I am letting Nikki borrow the diamond tennis bracelet he gave me for Christmas. Nikki is my girl and all, but holding on to six carats is not something that I would trust just anyone with. However, she begged me to let her borrow it. She's going to some dinner with her boyfriend for his job. She has the cutest little dress that she thinks the bracelet would just set off.

She's at the door now.

"Hey girlfriend, I knew your butt would be late."

"Girl, no one told you to move way out here. Michael is going to make sure nobody can get to you if you want to leave his crazy behind."

"You need to quit talking about my man."

"You're right. He's probably taping every damn thing you say and do while he is at work." Nikki has not gotten over the fact that I quit the squad because of Michael. She never passes up an opportunity to crack on him about being jealous.

Funny though she acts like they are best friends when he is around.

"Ok, I want my bracelet back first thing in the morning. I don't want Michael to miss it. Don't you dare take it off while you are out, or at a hotel."

"No, you did not. I'm still not convinced the damn bracelet is real. It probably has a tracking device hooked to it anyway, so crazy will know where you are at all times." She is cracking herself up. "You never did tell me why you were upset the other night when I called you."

"Girl, Michael was just acting a fool over something I had on when I went shopping that day. You know that cute, little, short dress with the scoop neck front that fits kind of snug? When he came home, he wanted to know if I wore it out. When I told him yes, he pitched a fit. He said since I can't figure out what is appropriate attire, he would do it himself. He ripped the dress off and threw it away. It just scared me that's all."

"That's all! Meeka, you had better start putting Michael in check. He thinks that he owns you. I would love to have a man that takes care of me the way that Michael takes care of you. You don't have to work, you have a nice home, and car, but it should not have to come with him trying to tell you what to do. What happens if you decide not to do something he tells you to do?"

"I don't really know. I mean we don't really fight about things. You know how you say I am so passive. A lot of things that may bother some people don't really bother me. If Michael does not want me to wear something, or go somewhere, it really does not bother me. I just don't do it."

"That's how it starts. I really can't give you much advice on your relationship because it's different than anything that I've ever been in. Yes, I've been involved with a married man before, but no one ever left their wife for me. Not that I wanted them to. Also, they would drop a few dollars, but damnit, you have the whole wallet. I do know that men that are jealous must either change or it usually gets out of hand. If you are okay and happy, so am I."

"And I am."

The garage door was going up and Michael was home.

I'm glad he came home a little early that way we can have dinner and some time together before he goes out to his card game. He and Nikki exchanged greetings and joked around some.

As soon as she left Michael made a smart comment about *this ain't no damn sorority house.*

He did not want to come home every day and see her sitting up in here.

I have all day to do what I wanted and needed to do. When he came home, he wanted some peace and quiet with me. While he was fussing, I helped him take off his clothes and gave him his *Meeka appetizer* before dinner.

I have learned how to calm Michael down.

I know exactly what he needs and how he likes it.

Chapter Twenty-Four

MICHAEL

Things couldn't be going any better. I made Partner at work this week. I've never considered myself a corporate type of guy, but it comes easy for me. I don't mind hard work—the engineering career is what I like and I'm very good at it.

It's kind of like gambling to me.

It's not hard and I win more than I lose.

While I'm working, I might as well be successful at it.

Diane signed the divorce papers today and there was no drama at court. David and I had a quick lunch afterwards and he told me that for all practical purposes I am a single man. If it was not for my relationship with Meeka, there's no telling what I would be doing tonight to celebrate, but even though I'm free on the one hand I'm very much committed on the other and this time around I like being committed. Meeka has been very patient and accommodating. I never once felt real pressure from her to even leave Diane. I just hope that the dynamics between her, her mother and Diane somehow withstand what's up ahead.

Todd's and Deena's wedding is this weekend. In talking with Todd, he mentioned that Diane was going to be a part of the wedding party. Deena had already asked her to be a hostess before the whole divorce ordeal started. Enough time since Diane signed the papers had not gone by to give any type of appearance that Meeka and I have connected since then. I don't think this is the right time for Meeka and me to be flaunting our relationship. I would hate to cause a disturbance at my boy's wedding, and I am the best man. I know Meeka will be pissed, but hopefully this will be the last of trying to be inconspicuous about our relationship. Since so many of the wedding party participants are coming in from out of town, the rehearsal will be early Friday. Todd's dad is doing an old fashion barbeque for the rehearsal dinner at his house. For as long as I can remember, Todd's dad has always loved to throw down at gatherings. We may get so caught up in the food and alcohol at the barbeque we won't make it for the plans I have later that night.

Meeka should have picked up my tuxedo by now and is back at the house. I guess this will be a better time than any to discuss how we should handle this weekend. I don't want to wait until Friday and discuss this because I don't want her making irrational emotional decisions during that time. That's the only thing about our age difference that I've noticed. Meeka's decision making can be totally off, especially when her emotions are involved.

As I open the garage, I think about how one day I'll be coming home not only to Meeka, but to our children as well. I can't believe how far I've come in being okay with having kids.

Meeka makes things easy, and I feel in control of our lives.

It's not hard to be comfortable and confident in a relationship when you have control over things. Not having control is what takes me out of my element. Baby girl is here. I know she was out earlier running errands and practicing. She is freaking out about her upcoming finals and the time she has had to practice this routine for the wedding. I'm trying to be supportive, but I want to tell her that since she is not going to work, the whole GPA thing is overrated. Even if she makes C's on all her exams, she would graduate with a B average.

As I slide my arms around her waist while she is fixing dinner, I hate to ruin the mood later in talking about this weekend. We have a great dinner and are lying around on the couch, when I broach the subject.

"Sweetheart, you know the wedding is this weekend. How do you want to go about the logistics?"

"What do you mean?"

"Well, we have the rehearsal and rehearsal dinner on Friday, and the wedding on Saturday. I was thinking it would probably not be a good idea for us to attend these functions as a couple, since the divorce just became final. Plus, Todd mentioned that Diane is in the wedding party." I could feel her body tense up against me. She sat up and looked at me with deeply hurt eyes.

"Michael, are you telling me that I'm supposed to go to this weekend's activities and act like we are not together and like I am dateless?"

"Baby, I swear I don't think the timing is right. Your parents will be there, and I know your mother does not want Diane to find out this way about us. It would just be a difficult situation on everyone."

"What about the situation I've been in Michael? What about how I've had to hide, as the woman you supposedly *love*. Do you think things have been easy for me?"

The last thing I wanted to do was to turn this discussion into an argument. I really was hoping that Meeka would understand and cooperate. I could see how far we had come and honestly, I did not think that things would not have blown up before now. Since it had not, I guess I was being optimistic that other relationships could be salvaged here.

"Meeka, I need you to think this through without all the emotion. What do you think will happen if we come popping up at the rehearsal holding hands in front of everyone?" When she stood up and folded her arms, I knew I was not about to get an emotionless response.

"I tell you what Michael. I think you should just go and by the way, pick Diane up and give her a ride. Oh, and stop by and ask my mother if she needs a damn lift to. They seem to be the only two people that you are thinking about. You can't possibly be thinking about me and how I feel, since you don't have a clue on how bad I've been hurting."

As she walked away and slammed the door to the bedroom, I started trying to figure where in the hell did the conversation take a turn in this direction.

I laid on the couch a couple of hours watching ESPN.

When I finally got up to go to bed, I turned the doorknob to the bedroom and the door was locked. Instead of kicking the damn door down and demanding that Meeka show me a payroll stub and cancelled checks on where she has been paying bills, I thought about my sister Tia and the advice she had given me on managing my temper. I tapped on the door and asked Meeka to open the door. When baby girl opened the door, I could tell she had been crying. I probably should have come straight in here when she first slammed the door, but I had gotten sucked into the Final Four series and before I knew it two hours had passed.

I felt bad that she had been in here crying.

"Meeka, listen. I know this is not easy sweetheart, but I'm really trying to make a tough situation turn out okay. If you have a better way of doing this, please let me know. By the way, if you don't care about the people's wedding we are in or your mother; then let's let the chips fall where they will this weekend."

She started crying again.

"Michael, I'm just tired. I just want to be with the man I love without any thought and or effort. I just want us to be free with each other. Sometimes I feel like the way we are living is okay with you."

"This is not okay with me. I am not getting anything out of this other than protecting you. Meeka, your mom is going to hate me even if she and Diane remain best friends or not. Diane is going to hate me as well and I don't care. I do care about my boy having the wedding he deserves without me messing it up with my drama, but not more than I love you baby. I'm just trying to do what I can."

When I pulled her close to me, I could tell she was hesitant. "Baby, please don't put a wall up between us." She looked up at me with those pretty eyes and my heart melted.

This girl is so sweet I really hate what I've put her through.

She deserves to be treated like the princess she is, not loved undercover. I put my hand under her chin and kissed her with every passionate fiber I had. I wanted her to know that the way things were was not optimal to me either. When I felt her tongue slide into my mouth, all I could think of was burying myself inside of her.

We moved to the bed, and she undressed me proving to me that she wanted me just as much as I wanted to be with her. I love her natural smell and the softness of her hair. Making love to her always feels new. I never have to think twice about anything I want to do to her when we make love. Knowing that

I am the only man that has touched her gives me a since of freedom and ownership with her body.

I had not planned on doing things this way, but I wanted to prove to her that my commitment to and for her was not in question. One thing I enjoy with Meeka is her expressions and body language when I'm loving her.

I can easily tell when she is about to explode and reach her climax.

As I was bringing her to her breaking point, I reached into the nightstand and pulled out the ring I had planned to give to her later. I was glad I had taken it out of the box previously.

It was easier to keep hidden in the side of the drawer that way.

I started thrusting her harder and harder so that I could share this moment of passion at the same time with her. I pinned her hands up above her head and her legs gripped me tightly. I heard her start crying my name and I slid the ring on her left finger. As we both came down, she must have felt something different on her hand. When she saw the ring, the tears started flowing down her face. I did not have to ask her anything and she did not have to respond. She knew she was going to be my wife.

Chapter Twenty-Five

Meeka

When I think back to the sports bar and how Michael and I connected, this love that we have is so unseemly. Who would have thought that my godmother's husband would be the man that fills my hearts capacity and calms my restless soul? Most women think of a love that will complete them, but so many settle. I have to confess that Michael's love is much more than I could have imagined. Maybe because it did not exist until we met. I have to say wearing a flawless six carat diamond ring does not make me want to cooperate any more with this weekend. I want to wear my ring with pride and stand next to my man, but I understand what Michael is talking about and I don't want to be the cause of any drama at Deena's wedding.

As I pull up into my parent's driveway, I am so excited about my engagement. Even if my mother is negative, at least she will know that Michael has the best intentions towards me. She was so furious at me for moving in with him, but it only made sense at the time.

"Hello, is anyone home?"

"Meeka, why are you acting like you've never lived here. Do you think anybody is home crazy?" My mother can be funny in her own way. She and my dad were sitting in the family room watching TV. When I came in, they looked up at me and gave me their normal smiles and greetings. I sat down on the couch and asked what they were doing. Again, smart-butt had to say they were on a camping trip. I wanted them to notice my ring, so I decided to just wait.

"Mom, do you know what you are wearing to Deena's wedding?"

"Girl, I have the cutest little peach dress that I bought the other day. I am debating on putting a hat with it. What do you think?" I ran my fingers threw my hair and their mouths dropped to the floor. Even my dad had an amazed expression on his face.

"Meeeeeeka, what is that on your finger?"

"Oh, this little thing. Michael gave it to me as some type of special ring……oh, I believe they call it an engagement ring!" As I was smiling ear to ear and beaming with all the love I have for Michael and how he makes me feel, I was expecting the same from my parents; however, I suddenly realized how much they hated Michael, and they were not happy one bit. My father tried to be diplomatic about things.

"Princess, don't you think you should take your time? Michael just got divorced and you guys have been together for less than a year. Initially, I thought moving in was a bad step, but at least you were not getting into a binding commitment."

Of course, my mother was less diplomatic. "Meeka, this is just too much! Diane's heart is broken in two and now you have the audacity to be wearing Michael's engagement ring. The damn ink is not even dry on the divorce papers and only God knows what's going to happen when Diane finds out that her beloved goddaughter was screwing her husband the whole time. You were not raised to be this insensitive and immoral."

I don't know why I expected a different reaction from my parents, but it was evident I would not have their support. Instead of saying something hurtful to them in retaliation for how I was feeling, I just stood up to leave. As the tears started rolling down my face, I thought: *here I am graduating in two months from college with excellent grades.* I've done everything my parents, and everyone else thought I should do. I fall in love with someone who I want to spend the rest of my life with and all they can do is find fault. I know this is not the ideal situation, but I don't think I would crush my daughter's happiness this way.

My father must have read my mind and my heart.

"Princess, don't go. I'm sorry your feelings are hurt. I'm sure you are very excited right now and would love for us to be excited with you. Meeka, I love you and your happiness is everything to me. You know your old man is struggling with your selection of a mate, but I'm willing to try to support you. It's not easy letting your baby make her own decisions. You can't be mad at me for loving you so much."

I fell into my daddy's lap and planted a kiss on the side of his cheek. I could see my dad was being sincere and I know he only has my best interest at heart. I did not feel the same way about my mother, as I know she was more concerned about Diane. All my mom could muster up was that the ring was gorgeous and at least Michael was more than able to care for me financially.

My mother asked when Michael and I planned to get married, and I told her we had not discussed a date yet. We started talking about graduation and Deena's wedding sweeping all the remaining issues under the rug as usual.

Chapter Twenty-Six

Meeka

The rehearsal starts at 1:00pm at the church. I was still not okay with the arrangements for the weekend, but I figured I would struggle through. The good thing is my dance routine was fabulous. I had really put a lot of effort into the choreography. I even had a few of the dancers I periodically partner with give me some ideas. I think I worked so hard on its perfection because it helped me get rid of the demons in my own life and I wanted to make Deena very happy.

I had already gone to the church a couple of times because I needed to get a feel for the layout of the area that I would be dancing in. I ran into the minister on my second visit. He was a younger pastor and we talked for a long time. He was very passionate about his ministry and commented on how passionate he could tell I was about dancing. He was a very handsome man and quite funny. As I was talking with him, I thought it would be nice to have him marry Michael and me. I did not mention it to him, but I just thought it would be nice. I really like how honest he seems to be. Most ministers put on such airs, that you feel uncomfortable being around them. Deena's pastor was just the opposite. I could have sat there and talked to him forever. I even forgot that he was a minister a couple of times. I told him how when Deena and I were little girls we would pretend to have bigger body parts than we ever ended up having. I would stuff socks in my shirt, and she would too. The two of us started laughing so hard that I forgot we were in the church. When he mentioned how women are always so self-conscious about their bodies, that if they spent just half that energy on their spirits they would be amazed at how at peace they would be; it was one of the sweetest things I had heard.

I think he was feeling equally comfortable with me. He said that the women in his church are always throwing themselves at him. He knows some ministers, especially the single ones, that take advantage of the cloth. He has no intentions of doing that. He sought long and hard to accept his calling as a minister. It's difficult enough to be so young, but to make a mockery of his calling was not something he would compromise in doing. He did say that a nice first lady is on his list of To Do's. I could really resonate with that; I cannot wait to be Michael's wife. I made a mental note to talk with Michael and see if he would like to use Deena's minister for our own wedding.

Diane and I attend the same church, so I don't think I would feel comfortable with my pastor marrying me. I've always been very close to Pastor James, but I know Diane has been crying in his office every day since Michael asked for a divorce. Pastor James did not marry them, but he did try and call Michael to counsel them to reconciliation. I'm not sure what Michael said, but he did not go, and Pastor James never called him again. I even remember once Diane going up front to the church asking that we pray that her husband would start coming to church with her. Half of the women in the church husbands were on the couch watching football, so there were amens and yes Lords all over the place.

My mother commented that if his black ass came in the church, it would fall down.

I had asked Michael when we got together why he did not go to church. He told me that he grew up in the church and sung in the choir as a young boy. As he got older, there were things he started to do that he felt he did not want to stop doing, so he stopped going to church because he felt it made him a hypocrite. I never really considered that perspective, but I told him it would mean a lot to me when we have a family that we go to church together. He did not say yes, but he did not say no either.

By the time I debated on wearing my ring or not, the not won. And, by the time I decided to drive or not drive my Lexus, I parked it and drove my other car. I was running late and feeling disgusted with myself. Michael had called and asked what was taking me so long. I told him why it mattered as we were not there together anyway. I'm not sure if his signal dropped, or he hung up on me. Either way, he did not call back and neither did I. When I walked in the church everyone was looking so damned happy. I hated it, but I was in the worst mood ever. It was not time for my cycle, but I could have smacked everyone in the wedding party. Deena's chicken looking butt was running around the church like she owned the place. I put on my fakest smile and gave her a big hug. I intentionally avoided eye contact with Michael. If I had looked at him, he would have probably dropped dead with the way I was thinking of him.

I sat down next to one of my cousins as the wedding coordinator went over the program and where everyone should be at the start. We were going to go through the rehearsal twice with the singing and dancing performances abbreviated. My dance was going to be once the bride and groom were at the altar. They would stand off to the side as I danced to "Greatest Love of All." I could feel Michael looking at me and I would not give him the satisfaction of even glancing over at him. I did see Diane staring at him like a lovesick puppy. Right about now, she could have him.

As we all stood up to go to our respective places, the minister came in and the coordinator commented on his perfect timing. He asked if we had opened the rehearsal with prayer and of course we had not. He laughed and asked us to hold hands with the person next to us. I can't believe it, but he came over to me and gave me a nice hug and kiss on the cheek. He took my hand and the coordinators and led us through prayer.

When I looked up, Michael was glaring at me, and I could tell he was pissed.

It did not help when Deena commented on how nice I would be as a First Lady. Although I did not want Michael to get the wrong impression, I could not help but think how it served him right to keep our relationship a secret.

I had to be the stand in for the bride during the rehearsal. Standing that close to the minister and Michael made me feel really nervous. I know how crazy Michael can get and I did not want his temper to get the best of him. Especially since the pastor was being extremely friendly to me. So, I decided to look up at Michael to give him a warm loving look from me during the vows. I think that pissed him off more, because he ignored me. Michael is really a spoiled little boy. Nikki is right about his jealousy. By now, he should know how much I love him and that I would never do anything with another man. It's probably a good thing that we can't really talk to each other because we would just be arguing anyway.

Michael had left the directions to Todd's father's house for me. After the rehearsal, I got in my car to go. I really was not sure that I wanted to attend the dinner this whole ordeal was taking a toll on my head. Not to even think that my parents would be coming to the barbeque. Todd's father is a sweetheart, he extended the rehearsal dinner out to just about everyone. He was having a catering company barbeque the food at his home. A couple of Michael's boys were also in the wedding party and were riding with him. I'm glad. I'm pretty sure I would have gotten an ear full if he was able to call me. I was all by myself and still feeling down about everything. I decided to run by the condo and take some aspirin. I sat on the couch to give the medicine time to kick in when my cell phone rang. Michael wanted to know where I was and what was taking me so long to get to the dinner. I told him I stopped by the condo. He had the nerve to accuse me of sleeping with the minister. We got into this big argument and Michael really hurt my feelings. He told me to quit acting like a child and get my spoiled tail to the dinner. Then he hung up on me.

When I got to the dinner, I could tell everyone was already having a great time. The bartender was very busy, and the guests were quite loud. I went straight to the bar to get a glass of wine. My head was still killing me, and I was hoping to find some kind of relief.

As I was walking away from the bar, I ran into Diane.

It was unavoidable, so I stopped and conducted small talk with her.

She seemed to be in good spirits and on her way to recovering from the breakup with Michael. When she started talking about how much she loved him and how he had treated her I wanted to run in the other direction; but all in all she was getting through the ordeal. I guess it would have been bad if Michael and I had been walking around hand in hand. She told me that Diamond should be here tomorrow and was planning on coming to the wedding. She would love it if the two of us could spend some time together.

She feels like Diamond could use a mentor right now to get her life on track.

I said if I had the time I would love to hang out with Diamond.

My mother came over and started talking with Diane and me.

I hated that one day Diane might not be speaking to either of us.

As we were talking, my eyes wondered around, and I saw Michael engaged with my cousin Sasha. Sasha is Deena's sister and the maid of honor. Her body language suggested that she was more than interested in Michael. She was showing every tooth she had in her mouth. I do have to give it to Sasha, growing up she always had a body that was extremely curvy. I remember asking my mother when I would get breasts and hips like Sasha's.

My mother said that I probably never would—she was right.

I really could not blame Sasha for anything because to everyone there, Michael was a new bachelor on the block. When she pulled him out on the makeshift dance floor, my heart sank. Even though it was a fast song, Sasha was bumping up against Michael as much as she could. The hurting part was that Michael seemed to be enjoying every moment of it.

Diane commented on how she noticed every female at the rehearsal and rehearsal dinner was after

Michael. She just knew his manhood was primetime right about now.

My mother gave me a *see what you have to look forward to* look.

I excused myself and headed back to the bar for glass of wine number two.

While I was waiting my turn at the bar, I heard a warm invite to dance. Chris looked so good in and out of the church surroundings. I was a little embarrassed standing at the bar and the minister was asking me to dance.

"Chris what are you doing here?" I still felt funny calling him by his first name, but he insisted when we were talking at the church.

"Well, I don't normally come to the rehearsal dinners of the people I'm going to marry the next day, but I figured you would be here and since you are such a great dancer you would teach me the latest moves."

I could not help but to laugh. I was thinking did he mean my majorette hoochie moves, or my church routines. Either way, I think he would look funny. When the bartender put my wine on the bar, I told him he got my order wrong that I wanted cranberry juice. Chris laughed so hard that he was holding his side.

"Meeka, it's okay for you to drink, I just don't. I don't want to make you nervous, so I promise after my dance I will leave."

"You don't have to leave, it's not like I am ashamed of who I am and what I do. I'm really a good person."

"I can tell, now what about my dance?"

Chris slid his hand in my hand and started for the dance area. I did not know how to tell him no, so I just followed behind. Michael and Sasha were still dancing, and a few other folks had joined them.

The DJ was playing Bruno Mars, "That's What I Like" and that is my jam.

I was amazed how smooth Chris was on the floor—he was a good dancer. I was enjoying our conversation and thought he was really a sweet guy. The way that he was looking at me made me feel a little nervous.

Nikki is always telling me how naïve I am when it comes to men.

They would pretty much have to hit me on top of my head for me to notice that they are interested. Chris is a cutie, but my heart belongs totally to Michael.

I do think it would be good to introduce him to Nikki. Chris may be someone who could slow her down and appreciate her for all her wonderful qualities. The guy she was seeing now was okay, but Chris would be much better for her. Chris interrupted my train of thought when he asked me if I was seeing anyone. I really did not want to lie to a minister, but if I said yes, he would probably follow up with a lot of other questions like what's his name and why was he not with me.

I figured I'd have to lie anyway at that point, so I said no.

The next song that came on was a slow jam, so I thanked Chris and started to walk off the dance floor. I noticed Michael was doing the same thing and that was a relief. Chris followed behind me and asked if it would be okay to call me some time. I explained to him that I had a lot going on in school and I had a made a conscience decision not to date until I graduated and landed a job.

He was so respectful and kind he said he could appreciate my decision.

He told me that I knew how to find him and not to wait too long, he was having a hard time keeping the women parishioners away. We both laughed and he said he would see me on tomorrow.

He gave me a nice hug and left.

My mother broke her neck trying to get over to me and ask me a million questions about my minister friend. In annoyance, I explained to her that Chris was just someone I met, and I had no interest in him whatsoever.

I love and am engaged to Michael.

The mention of his name sent her in another direction.

It was after 9:00pm and I ended up having a nice time. When I was about to leave, Deena came over and asked if I was coming to the bachelorette party. I told her that I was not really planning on it, and she seemed hurt.

"I can't believe my own cousin is dancing in my wedding and is not going to celebrate with me through the night."

Sasha chimed in and said that she was trying to get the location of the bachelors' party out of Mr. Fine Ass Michael, so we could merge the two.

It was hard to sit there while she talked about my fiancé's anatomy and what she wanted to do with him. Although she did not incriminate Michael at all, I could tell he did not douse her hopes any during their conversation. I told Deena that I would try and meet them at the hotel later and that I was going home to shower and change. Once I had said my goodbyes, I headed toward my car. Michael was standing out front with Todd and some other guys and told me to hold up.

I could tell he had been smoking weed because his eyes were blood shot red.

I hated when he drank and got high because he was either super sweet or super hateful—with everything that had happened today, I knew which one he would be.

Chapter Twenty-Seven

MICHAEL

I was so pissed my head was killing me. I felt like I needed to explode, but the lid was on so damn tight I had to keep everything in. The whole time I was walking Meeka to the car I kept thinking about the church incident and her dancing with that guy. I don't care if he was the Pope, Meeka knows better than to do what she did.

Why is she driving this ragged ass car anyway and where was her engagement ring?

When I grabbed a hold of her arm, I guess I did not realize how firm of a grip I had on her. She winced and tried to pull away, which made me grip her tighter.

"Michael, you are hurting me!"

I could tell she was afraid and rightly so.

Did she think I would be okay with the stunt she pulled tonight?

"Shut up! Help me understand what you were trying to prove tonight with the minister and why in the hell did he feel comfortable enough to kiss on you?" I really did not want to cause a scene, but if

Meeka started crying and did not answer me, we were going to have some major problems tonight.

"Michael, I had met him at the church when I went to practice there before. He was only being friendly and did not mean anything at all. You are scaring me and hurting my arm, please stop."

One of my boys was looking towards me and I let Meeka go.

This undercover stuff was becoming too much, but good thing for her I had no intentions of ruining this time for Todd and Deena. I told Meeka to go home, and I would deal with her when I got there. I had planned on showering and changing before I went to the bachelor's party and would be right behind her.

This felt like the longest drive of my life, even though it was only thirty minutes away. I'm doing all I can to prove my love to this girl and I am not going to tolerate this nonsense.

For some reason the other morning, I woke up kind of early. The sun was coming up and Meeka was still asleep. I looked over at her and had the most conflicting emotions I've ever experienced. I had the deepest sensation of love I've never felt for another human being and at the same time I felt completely powerless. It's hard to describe, but Meeka makes me strong and weak at the same time. I'm not sure what to do with these feelings, but I've got to get a hold of myself.

When I walked into the house, she had turned on the lights and I saw that her arm was bruised. She was frightened as hell because she kept running her fingers through her hair and fidgeting. I was still very upset, but something about seeing her looking at me with so much fear made me calm down. I explained to Meeka that if I did not love her so much, then I would probably care less about what she did or who she did it with. I feel like no matter how much I communicate to her what I'm trying to do and how much I am trying to protect her that she is not getting it. This is so frustrating, and it does not help to see my fiancé being kissed or hugged by another man I don't care who he is. I know the situation is equally difficult for her and I own some of the responsibility of what happened tonight. If it had been evident that Meeka had a man, then maybe the good Reverend would not have felt as comfortable demonstrating his interest in her.

I was not sure if she understood what I was trying to say, or she was agreeing with me out of fear. I don't want her to be afraid of me. My temper sometimes gets the best of me, but I've been working on it with Meeka. The last thing I want to do is have a physical confrontation with her. I don't plan on losing her for any reason. When she mentioned my talking and dancing with Sasha should not have happened either, I told her she was right, but I guess I stepped out of bounds reacting to what happened during the rehearsal. I assured her that I had no interest in Sasha and that she should know by now that she's got me wrapped up tight. The things that I've done for Meeka are a first and no woman has ever captured my heart or complete attention like she has.

"Meeka, I think it's time you came off birth control. I want us to start working on having a baby."

She looked surprised.

She told me that she loved me and wanted to have a baby with me, but she felt that that should happen after our wedding.

I told her that was fine—we'll just go to Vegas next week and get married.

"Michael, I don't want a wedding in Vegas. I want a real wedding with my family and friends. I've always wanted a church wedding with the man I love."

"You can't have everything your way Meeka. I want you pregnant. If you can plan the wedding of your dreams in nine months then fine, but I want you off the pill immediately." I can't explain the way I was feeling, but I did not like the idea of losing control over our relationship and I felt that a baby would help settle things down. I know how we both felt about losing the baby and how close we were at that point.

It was getting late, and I did not want to get into an argument about anything else. I told Meeka we would talk about it later. After the night we had, I thought it was best if Meeka stayed at home and not attend Deena's bachelorette party. I really don't like her out late at night and I certainly don't want her putting my hard-earned money in some guy's G-string. She said she would just call Deena and leave a message on her voice mail that she was not able to attend. I went to shower and get changed so I could get to the club before Todd arrived. I gave Meeka a kiss and told her not to wait up on me, but I would have my cell on if she needed me.

The strip joint that all the fellas were going to meet at use to be a regular for me. The girls look decent, and the music is always off the chain. I had reserved the VIP area and made sure that all the alcohol and appetizers we would need were ordered. It was about thirty guys at the party, and we were all drunk after about the first hour and a half. Todd was feeling pretty good. I don't think I've ever seen him so loose. A couple of dancers had come up to our area and was entertaining the guys.

One of the girls was this hottie name Tammy.

She had a fine body and knew exactly what to do with it.

I don't need to pay for sex, but let's just say that a few times Tammy's private lap dances turned into her sliding her thongs completely off and taking a ride to pleasure me. I know she enjoyed me as much as I did her. Whenever I was at the club, she always seemed to find me. We went to her place a few times, but getting involved with a stripper was not on my list of things to do before I died.

When Tammy came over to me tonight, screwing her was the last thing on my mind. I was eager for this set to start winding down, so that I could get home to my baby. I politely told Tammy that her attention should be focused on Todd since he was the man of the hour. Surprisingly enough I saw Todd follow Tammy to the back for a private lap dance. I can't imagine that he would do anything else, but a brother would never ask.

It was about 4:00am when I got home. Meeka was in the bed asleep. I hated to crawl in the bed smelling like smoke and alcohol, but I was too drunk to even think about taking a shower. As soon as I crawled in the bed and felt her up against me, I had to have her before I went to sleep.

Either she was extremely tired or was just not welcoming my advances.

"Baby girl, I missed you tonight." I rubbed my hands down the side of her thighs.

"It's not tonight, Michael, its tomorrow."

Oh, she's upset because I was out late.

I know she understands that a bachelor's party did not have time constraints.

"Sweetheart, I'm sorry the time got away from me. Since I am the best man and was throwing the party, I could not just up and leave. Let me make love to you baby and show you how much I've been missing you." When she rolled over and wrapped her arms around my neck, I pulled up her night gown and felt the softness of her body against my hand. I was too drunk to have a lot of foreplay, but Meeka must have been missing me because she was moist already and did not require much.

I enjoy her body so much that I don't think I would survive if she ever took it away from me. I made sure she enjoyed the full pleasure of her man and after we had finished exchanging love, I fell fast asleep.

Chapter Twenty-Eight

Meeka

I believe I have completely lost myself in this man. I cannot figure out when I lost the ability to reason for myself. Everything I seem to think or feel revolves around what Michael thinks or feels. The things that I thought were completely unacceptable in a relationship seemed to have blurred now that I am in one with this man that I love so much. If someone had asked me if it's okay for a man to scare a woman in their relationship or make her feel intimidated I would have immediately without hesitation said no.

Who have I become?

I was not the young woman who would get involved with a married man, become pregnant by him and move in with him before being married. I was confident, decisive, and very focused. Now the only focusing that I do is to make sure that Michael is happy and cared for. I don't think that is a bad thing since I am going to be his wife, but I'm not sure if that's the only thing that I should be doing.

Now I understand why Diane could not leave Michael.

He's not the type of man you just leave.

You're so obsessed with him that you don't dare want another woman to have him. The thought of someone enjoying what he has to offer of what is truly good about him is incomprehensible. Even when he is not the good man that you love so much, you are so deep into him that you absolve him of any of his negative characteristics and charge them to your own account. Questioning yourself as to what have you done wrong to make Michael be that way? Love is not a good word to describe how I feel about Michael, but there is not one that I know of that is universal enough to explain my feelings.

I hope I can one day though.

I've become one with the music and each movement that I make seems to be perfect. It is like I am supposed to be moving my body this way, at this time, in this wedding. In my slow turns, I see Deena dabbing her eyes. It's only because I see myself nine months from now dabbing my own eyes in the same place that she stands in.

I can't help but to cry now.

My soul is embracing every emotion that I've had over the past several weeks and exploding at this very moment in this church under the words of this beautiful song. I see my heart standing next to Todd and I know that I am meant to be with Michael.

There is no other place to be, nor other man to be with.

I've shared the very essence of who I am with him and given to him the better part of me. Other's must be feeling the same way I'm feeling because as I take my bow, there seem to be more people crying than not. I look over at Michael and even his eyes are moist.

The rest of the wedding ceremony is beautiful. The church was decorated so beautifully. Deena chose rose gold and ivory for her color scheme. There were ivory flowers alternated by each pew in large rose gold vases. Her wedding party had rose gold dresses and the groomsmen wore ivory tuxedos with rose colored bow ties.

Todd and Deena exchange custom vows and they seem so much in love. Now that Mr. Johnson has given me the blueprint to my future to plan a wedding in nine months or have a baby out of wedlock; I was planning my wedding through most of Deena's. I don't want to be pregnant or at least not showing during my own wedding, so the latest date will have to be in July. That means I will be studying for finals, graduating from college, and getting married and may be even pregnant over the next four months.

This is just like Michael to be so demanding and impatient.

As the wedding party exits, Michael glances over at me and we exchange smiles. After all these months, I still melt when he looks at me and smiles. I know that I will arrive at the reception late because I will need to shower and change. The intensity of my dancing always causes me to perspire. I dare not put on my dress without showering. As the guest file out of the church, I see Diane and her date leaving. I think my mother had mentioned she was dating someone from work--I'm glad for her.

Who knows she may like him enough to forgive me for getting involved with Michael—stranger things have happened, and I think our complex relationship is proof of just that.

On my way back to the women's changing area, I run into Chris. He tells me that he was moved to tears with my performance. He questioned where a woman of my age could ever find all the emotions that I demonstrate in my dancing. I opened my mouth to try and explain, but all I could do was cry. Oddly enough he did not ask me anymore questions, he just hugged me. I think I cried in his arms for ten minutes before I pulled away and told him that I needed to get changed and get over to the reception. He gave me the gentlest smile and told me anytime I wanted to talk to come by and see him.

Chapter Twenty-Nine

MICHAEL

Man, Meeka will make a brother turn into a crybaby with that dancing. She is like a stranger when I see her dancing like that. I've always enjoyed seeing her move, but in this case, it was not about her body so much as the atmosphere she creates. I could tell she was releasing some emotions that she had pinned up as well. The tears that were streaming down her face made me want to hold her and promise to be a better man for her. She's been through so much and I know being with me has not been easy. In my thirty years, I've never sat around thinking about how to be a better man or make someone happier.

With Meeka, taking care of her is my number one priority.

I can certainly understand why Meeka would want to have a wedding. It was nice seeing Deena and Todd exchange their vows and commit their love to each other publicly. I think ceremonies have more meaning when the people in them really have the feelings they are confessing.

When I looked out into the audience and saw my ex with her date, I was glad our experience did not turn her against the male species. Diane just needs to find someone that she fits with. My mother and Tia looked nice. They too were crying during Meeka's performance. Although Meeka has not officially met them, I know they will love her just as much as I do. I did point Meeka out to Tia before the wedding started. Tia's crazy butt was talking about how cute her nephews and nieces were going to be. I must agree, not so much because of me, but because of how beautiful Meeka is.

I can't wait to get her pregnant.

I decided to pass on the limo ride to the reception. Me and one of my boys who was also a groomsman rode in my car. When I pulled out of the church parking lot, I saw the Lexus SUV still there, so I assumed Meeka was changing and would be heading over. I almost turned around to wait on her to make sure that the good Reverend was not trying to push up on her, but after our argument last night I decided that I really need to try and get a grip on this jealous thing. Conceptually, I know I have no reason to be jealous when it comes to Meeka. She has proven her love and commitment to me repeatedly. For her to agree to getting pregnant and trying to plan a wedding in the interim shows how much she wants to be with me. We took the long route to the reception and smoked a joint. When we got there, we stood outside a couple of minutes to air out and try to clear our heads.

When I walked into the reception hall Sasha was looking all pissed. She said she and the other chick had to walk in and be announced by themselves because we were not there to escort them in.

I told her I did not realize this was the damn prom.

She made me promise to dance with her and she would think about forgiving me. Evidently Deena was pissed too because she tried to be smart and asked me if I thought I could fulfill the rest of my best man responsibilities without totally screwing up her wedding day. Todd was laughing and I told him the laugh was on him. This is just a taste of what he could expect now that he said I do. Deena rolled her eyes and walked away.

I must admit Deena has great taste. The reception hall was amazing. There was soft music being played by a live band. She also had DJ setup. Every table had an ivory tablecloth and a flower centerpiece with pink roses. The entire place was illuminated by candles. It was not a large venue but in the center was a dance floor. All the seating was arranged in tables of four or tabletops for two or three. The head table sat at the front of the Hall, where the wedding party would sit. It was a work of art. I know women love weddings, but I may have some ideas too.

As I made my rounds meeting and greeting folks, I felt like a magnet for women. I never really paid attention to the way women threw themselves at me because it felt natural. Even while I was married to Diane, women just did not seem to care. They were a little more inconspicuous, but still they were after a brother. I think I noticed it more now, because I did not want to do anything to make Meeka feel uncomfortable. I think I finally understood how she has been feeling having a man that she could not be open about. I felt that same way at the reception.

I stopped by Diane's table and met Jerome. Diane must not have gone into detail on how horrible our marriage was because Jerome was shaking my hand like I was the prime minister of somewhere. Mack and Linda were sitting at the same table, and I greeted them like I had not just seen them earlier today at the house when they stopped by so that Linda could work her magic on pinning Meeka's hair up into this tight ball that I hate.

I told Meeka to take that shit down as soon as she finished dancing.

She looked like my second-grade teacher Mrs. Dixon.

I had gotten me some cognac and was chillin' near the wedding party's table when Meeka walked in.

Damn, she looked so good.

I've been with her for a while now, why does she always look so new to me.

I want to meet her every time I see her—sometimes I have to remind myself that she is already mine.

She had on this short, black, halter dress that was slightly fuller at the bottom. I could tell that she did not have a bra on, but her breasts are so perky and small that she never really has to wear one. Although I tease her on how tiny she is, her legs are thin but muscular—and with those black, red-bottom heels, I would love to have those legs wrapped around my neck right about now.

When she turned around, the way her hair fell to the small of her bare back instantly aroused me. When our eyes connected, we exchanged smiles, but she looked sad. I know she hates attending all these activities alone. I think we are both ready to get on with our lives. She went and had a seat at the table with Sasha and some of the other ladies.

Chapter Thirty

MEEKA

If there is one thing I can say, Michael is the most handsome man I have ever seen. In a tuxedo, his finesse goes off the charts. What woman would not want to be standing next to him, soaking up all the attention he has to offer? Anytime he wears black, his eyes dominate every aspect of his appearance. He has the perfect physique to dress up or down. I think he knows it because his half of the closet is just as full as mine, but I know he likes nice things. It breaks my heart that I have to be here and pretend not to know him the way that I do.

My body wants to be next to him.

My waist longs to have his arm wrapped around me claiming me as his own.

It's crushing me to see all the women cheesing in his face trying to catch his eye. When our eyes meet, I try to muster up a smile, but really all I want to do is cry. I would not dare sit by my parents and Diane. I take a seat with Sasha and some other ladies. This one woman is talking about how fine Michael is and who is he with. Another woman comments that he is recently divorced and is on the market. She has yet to see him with anyone. Sasha chimes in and says that he will be with her tonight if she has her way. Everyone starts giggling and I cough up a fake laugh.

The wedding coordinator comes up front and announces that it is time for the bride and groom to take their first dance as Mr. and Mrs. Todd Waddell. The song that plays is one that I love, and Michael and I have been in bed making love to on several occasions. I don't think I'll be able to stomach this too much. Deena is so happy, and Todd is grinning ear to ear with his new bride.

They deserve to be happy.

After a few minutes into the song, Michael starts walking over to the table. It dawns on me that its customary for the best man and maid of honor to dance, especially if the father of the bride is not there. I'm fighting back the tears that I want to flow and kicking myself for even sitting next to Sasha. When Michael extends his hand out in front of me, I look into his eyes and realize he knows exactly what he is doing. I did not think that I would be able to walk out onto the middle of the floor without breaking down, but when Michael puts his hand in the small of my back and guides me to the dance floor, I know I will be okay.

I can feel everyone's eyes on me as Michael takes my hands and lifts them up around his neck. At this point, our eyes are locked. I believe he can sense all the love that I have for him because he softly smiles at me. As he slides his hands around my waist and pulls me against him, the very smell of his essence calms me instantly. I am in a familiar place with a man that holds my heart with his.

"You okay, baby girl?"

"Michael, I'm more than okay being right here with you."

"Are you sure you are ready to do this thing?"

I knew exactly what he meant, and I was never more ready to do anything in my life. Whatever had to happen I was okay with it because I would be with Michael.

"Yes, baby."

When Michael tilted my chin up to face him and lowered his lips to mine, I felt like this was my wedding day. My day to stand before the world with the man I love and announce our commitment together.

Michael's tongue was soft and moist—it almost felt like our first kiss. As I caress the back of his neck, I feel him growing up against me. That is one thing, my baby has no shame when it comes to his desire for me, and I like it. I think we must have kissed for five minutes before we let each other go. The sadness I felt earlier was replaced with happiness. When Michael reached in the inside of his jacket pocket and pulled out my engagement ring, I remembered that I had left it at home on the dresser because I did not want to draw attention to myself. He took my left hand and slid the ring on. Tears were sliding down my face and I did not dare try to wipe them. Michael brushed his lips against mine.

"Meeka, I want you to stay next to me for the rest of the night baby."

"Is there any other place for me to be?"

As we walked off the floor hand in hand, I saw Todd smiling at us.

Chapter Thirty-One

MICHAEL

That was my song. There was no way in hell I was going to dance with Sasha and leave my baby sitting there alone. She looked so sad, and I knew what I needed to do to let her know she is my everything. When I was leaving the condo, I noticed Meeka had put her ring on the dresser, at the time I was not sure what I was going to do with it, but I'm glad I picked it up. I don't care what anybody says that gambling instinct pays off when you listen to it.

When we left the dance floor, Tia's butt came running over dragging my mother with her. She was introducing my moms to Meeka like she already knew her. Baby girl was glowing. My mother knows good people when she sees them. She hugged Meeka and welcomed her to our family. I did not want to take too much away from Todd's thing, so I asked Tia to chill with all the commotion. I will bring Meeka to the house tomorrow for her to run the damn twenty questions by her. I was looking around to ensure people were in their proper places and Diane was not about to catch me off guard. I did not see her or Jerome anywhere, but Linda was coming our way looking like she had just found a used band aid in her salad. I was not about to have Linda negate the happiness that both Meeka and I were feeling.

When she asked could she speak to Meeka alone.

I politely, but firmly told her no.

Whatever you or anyone else needed to talk to Meeka about can wait until tomorrow. As quickly as she scurried her ass over to us, she turned and made her way back to Mack. I could not be sure, but Mack appeared to have this smirk on his face that indicated he was happy that Meeka was so happy.

The wedding coordinator came back up and announced that we would be having the toast for the bride and groom. As they passed out the champaign, I took that as an opportunity to grab another quick kiss from Meeka. This was an interesting kiss. I got all teeth. Baby girl cannot stop beaming. I had to laugh and so did she.

The rest of the reception went smoothly.

I kept Meeka next to me and kept my arms wrapped around her as much as possible. We decided to get a room at the hotel afterwards instead of driving to the condo. I'm glad Todd and Deena was on the honeymoon floor and not on our floor. I would have hated to show Todd up on his honeymoon night. Meeka and I did some headboard banging for about two hours that night.

Chapter Thirty-Two

Meeka

Last night was so wonderful. It truly felt like a burden had been lifted from my shoulders. Loving someone so deeply and not being able to acknowledge those feelings in the opening has been very difficult. Michael made me feel like the most important person in his world last night. The unfortunate thing is that it has opened the door to Michael and I having to face the people that we hurt.

When I turned my cell phone on this morning, Diane had left me fifteen angry and degrading messages. She rambled on about me being a home wrecker and a back-stabbing whore.

I was so hurt by her comments.

I really don't know what I was expecting, but the venom in her words stung so deeply. Michael turned his cell phone on and had double the number of irate messages that I did. He did not appear to be as bothered by them as I was. He told me to give it a few days and see if she would settle down. In my gut, I knew that it would take more than a few days. I did not tell him the last message she left had a threatening tone and she had informed me that we would be speaking face to face. If I had the nerve to fuck a married man, her husband; then I should have the nerve to confront her. I wanted to check on my mother and see if she had heard from Diane. Michael told me to wait a few days on talking to her as well. He just felt like there needed to be some time to pass between events.

I agreed.

I have to admit, Michael was right. Our "coming out" caused a lot of craziness. One of my cousins told me that Sasha was even mad at me. Not sure how Michael being the best man turned into him being her man. She was obviously delusional in thinking there was more between them, just because he danced with her at the rehearsal dinner. I really hope all of this settles down soon. I just want to be in a normal relationship with the man I love and move forward with our lives.

The next day we went by his parent's home. His mother and father were so nice. I could see a resemblance of both in Michael. His father was very laid back and seemed like the type that was not easily unnerved. I could tell in his day he probably had the women falling all over him just like Michael does. His mother is beautiful, but most of all she was genuinely kind. I had been concerned about what she would think of me. I'm sure she knew I had become involved with Michael during his marriage. If she did, she did not make me feel uncomfortable at all. She gave me a warm embrace when we arrived.

His sister Tia came over and was just as crazy as her brother—it was obvious that Michael adores his sister.

Although she too was extremely nice, I could tell she was checking me out the whole time.

It was so nice to hear his family talk about Michael in his younger years. I was so used to hearing my mother's evil comments, that hearing about Michael as a teen was refreshing. His mother said that he was a smart boy, but she could not control him to save her life. He would hang out all times of the night and when he was at home the phone rang off the hook so much for him, that she was surprised she never had a nervous breakdown.

Tia talked about how Michael had her stupid high school friends wanting him.

They both joked about the love-hate relationship Michael had with his brother over the women. His brother and family were out of town, but I would meet them real soon.

When it was time to leave, I figured that I must have passed the family inspection because Tia wanted to know when we were planning on getting married. I could not believe Michael was still on this nine-month kick. He told his family that we would be married within nine months as we are starting to work on a baby. I was so embarrassed until I saw the smile on his mother's face. Evidently, being a grandmother was very important to her. I wish I could have this type of support from my parents. The visit with the Johnson's just confirmed for me how much I wanted to have children. Being the only child has its perks, but being part of a family like this lends us to having more love to spread around.

I'm glad I finally had a chance to meet Michael's family and be recognized as someone he loves.

***

It's been six days since Diane's voice mail rampage. I felt as if I was constantly looking over my shoulder. I've never been threatened before and especially by someone who knew so much about me. Just the fact that she knew where I attended school, parent's information and so much of my business made me totally uncomfortable. I think Jerome was just a wedding date because her reaction to Michael and I being together was evidence that she was nowhere near over her marriage.

Michael is planning on going out to play cards tonight. I'm used to his Friday night games, but I would feel much more comfortable if he stayed in with me. He was pleased about us setting our wedding date for July, so I figured he would give in to me.

"Baby, do you really need to go out tonight gambling? With what happened last Saturday, I'm not feeling totally comfortable being home by myself so late." Michael is usually out to 2:00am on Friday nights.

"Meeka, you will be just fine. Diane was just blowing steam. She has not called you since, has she?"

"No, but I still don't feel totally safe. I did not mention that I think I've seen her car several times in places that I was going to or leaving from. I never actually saw her, so just thought I was being paranoid. I talked with my mother the other day and she said that Diane even exploded on her. She really thinks that we've pushed Diane over the edge."

My mom is really upset with me, but I'm glad she is at least acting like a mother. Through all of this, I never really knew where her loyalties lied. She spent so much time condemning me for getting involved with Michael that I felt like she cared more about her friendship with Diane than her own daughter.

However, when I finally talked with my mom, she told me that Diane called her really speaking badly of me. She said that she tried to empathize with her because she knew that Diane was feeling a lot of hurt and betrayal. She was hoping that she could still be a friend to Diane, especially since it sounded like once Diane found out how late my parents came to know about Michael and me that she did not seem to hold it against my mother. But my mother said, Diane was either a little too comfortable, or a little too angry because the bitch and whore references about me were a bit much.

My mother told Diane that I was still her baby and regardless of the choices I made, she would not have anyone talking about her daughter in that way. When she told me that she also told Diane that she owned some of the responsibility for her marriage ending, I was really surprised. My mother said before she hung up on Diane that she told her that I did not break up her messed-up marriage. That her marriage was over the first time Michael cheated on her and that should have let her know right then and there that he did not want her. They have not talked since.

Michael took me into our bedroom and between the mattress on his side he pulled out a 9MM. I could not believe he thought I would shoot my freaking godmother. He started trying to show me how to take the gun off the safety.

"Michael, have you lost your mind? I'm not going to use a gun on Diane or anyone else. You know I hate the fact that you have those things in the house. Instead of trying to teach me "How to Murder 101", please just stay at home with me."

"Meeka, I'm not going to be able to stay at home and babysit you forever, so tonight might as well be the night you get over your fear. I'll have my cell phone on, and I'll be home early, okay? Plus, the way you are talking about how you want this wedding, I hope I'm wrong, but I don't think Mack has planned to drop that much cash. I need to make some money."

I was not sure if Michael was really trying to help me get over my fear, or if he just needed his gambling fix. We've had some heated conversations about that in the past and I've let it go. Mainly because I hate to argue and plus, he is good at what he does. I just don't want it to come back to haunt us in the future. You can't win forever.

"Ok Michael, I'll be fine."

Michael left around 10:00pm. I decided to watch TV and try to stay up until he got home. I parked myself downstairs in the living area. One thing I love about this floor plan is how open and spacious the main living area is. I could see the kitchen, formal eating area and out to the deck area, which made me feel I had things covered. Our bedroom and office were right across from where I was sitting on the couch, so half of the house was in viewing range. I pulled out my wedding planner and started making notes for everything I would need to get done. The pressure was already mounting on me. My mother and Michael both suggested a wedding coordinator, but I am not hearing it. This is my special day and I want to plan every single aspect of it, so that everything has meaning.

I had scratched the idea of Chris marrying us. That would be super uncomfortable for everyone. I'm sure Michael would not have allowed it anyway. I also want a grander church to be married in. I was able to secure a Catholic church in a nice intimate adjoining town to the city we lived in. Although not a huge edifice, it would hold about 150 guests. The glossy wood floors and stained windows were the most adorable I've ever seen.

We are not catholic, but I've always loved their churches.

There were lots of gold accents in the church and the wood pews had a peach tone to them. I was really surprised the church allowed rentals and was open to having other ministers use the pulpit. The drive was about 40 minutes west. It would be a beautiful, serene drive by lots of trees and parks that would hopefully put our guest in a headspace of calmness. No wedding planner would have thought of that. I also love Michael in black. The ivory tuxedo was nice, but in black his eyes would be dazzling. My favorite color is pink, but that was too close to Deena's rose gold, plus I wanted a color that would pop with the natural wood décor of the church. I chose peach. I mentioned it to Nikki. Of course, she wanted red, but I shut that down quick.

Michael hates my hair up, but this is one fight he won't win. The wedding dresses that I'm looking at are conservative but having my back out is a must. Having my hair down would take away from the look I'm going for in the dress. The planning is a lot but it's going to be worth it.

A couple of hours later, I started feeling silly with all the lights on; so, I got up to start turning them out. Since all the main rooms are downstairs, it is usually completely dark upstairs in the loft area and the other two bedrooms and bath. I don't normally go upstairs, but when I looked up in the loft area, I saw a glimmer of light. As I walked around the kitchen and started up the stairs, I was wondering when did Michael come up here? The stairs land into the loft area and you can see over into the family room. There's an empty bedroom off to the left that adjoins with a Jack and Jill bath into the third bedroom. We do have some exercise equipment in there, but neither of us has been using it. I crossed the loft area and went into the bathroom. I noticed that the light in the walk-in closet in the bedroom was on. Not sure why I was feeling nervous, but I started toward the closet door. I hit the light switch and was standing in total darkness. A sudden fear engulfed me, and I ran out of the room and down the stairs. When I reached the bottom of the stairs, I kinda giggled to myself.

I really need to quit watching so much television.

I turned Michael's light off in his office. We had talked about if we were still here once I got pregnant that we would move his office upstairs and turn this room into the nursery. Michael wants to build a house and move, but with everything else going on there is no way I could manage that. For once, he agreed with me and said we could wait until after the wedding.

When I rounded the corner to go into our room, I heard the garage door go up. I felt a sigh of relief. I knew Michael said he would be home early, but I did not think he meant by midnight. I immediately ran to the door that leads out to the garage to greet him. There are four steps that lead up from the garage to the door.

Once I opened the door, I was frightened to see Diamond and Diane standing in my garage. Diane had this crazed look in her eyes, and I could not see her hands clearly. Diamond was at the bottom of the step closest to the door, and although I always thought how stupid the victims in scary movies seemed to me, I could not move.

Diamond started to talk but I could not take my eyes off of Diane. She looked so tired and unkempt.

I've never seen her look this way. It was as if she had not slept in weeks. He eyes were hollow and cold.

"Meeka, I know it's late, but we need to speak to you."

I must have been looking at her with complete confusion and fear on my face. She just started talking as if to catch me up to something that had happened that left me very far behind.

"When I got home tonight, my mother was sitting in our family room in the middle of the floor crying her eyes out. She is so depressed that I don't know what to do for her. I have to go back to school, and I don't want to leave her like this. I think she was really on her way to being over Michael, but now that her own goddaughter has hurt her, this is more than she can bear. I know you, Meeka. We are very different people, but we spent enough time together that I know what type of person you are. You would not intentionally and without regard do something like this to my mother, your godmother. I was hoping that maybe if the two of you talked and you explained your side of things, hopefully my mother could find some closure to all this pain she is feeling."

"Diamond, it's after midnight and you guys sneak into my garage and scare the hell out of me. Your mother has threatened me, and you want me to believe that all you want to do is talk to me."

"See mom what I told you. Meeka is so scary and timid there's no way she could have the heart to steal Michael maliciously. Look, Meeka, there's no way that Michael's controlling self would let us call you and make an appointment to meet with you. I also did not think I could walk up to your front door and ring the bell, without your scary tail freaking out and maybe calling the cops."

Diamond was right, there is no way I would have spoken with them if they had just showed up, and if they had called, Michael would not have let me meet with them.

"How did you and Diane get into our garage?"

In case you have not noticed, gamblers are habitual. The same four digits Michael uses for voice mail, security code, and bank pin are the same he would use for his garage door opener. We took a chance that he had not changed it. Just like when he goes out to gamble every Friday night."

"How did you find out where we lived?"

"Meeka, does it really matter? My mother has caller ID and Michael had called one day about some stuff he needed to pick up. My mother took the number and googled it to get his address. I'm not here to hurt you and I hope that after you talk with my mother that she can escape some of the hurt she has been feeling."

My demeanor softened and I looked at Diane and asked her what did she want to know? Her response was so low and weak that I could barely hear her, but it was clear enough to bring tears to my eyes. She had whispered how could I have done this to her?

As my own eyes filled with tears, I sat down on the steps in the garage.

I really did not know where to start, so I started with how I felt about her.

I explained to her that I have always loved her and appreciated her for everything she's done for me. I told her that Diamond is 100% correct in that I would never intentionally hurt her. My relationship with Michael evolved out of my feelings for him and not my disregard for her. Michael and I had not been conducting some secret love affair over the past four years behind her back. I never thought of Michael that way and he never came on to me. I told her that we had coincidentally run into each other. We started talking and got to know each other in a way that we never had before in other settings. We discovered an attraction that was all consuming. No matter how wrong I knew it was, I could not pull away from him.

I did not want to hurt her further, but I needed her to understand how much I loved Michael. I told her that I would do anything in the world not to hurt her, but even if I had to do it all over again, there's no way I could not fall in love with Michael. Oddly enough, I think she understood. She too had felt that way about him.

Diane did not have much in response other than she did not hate me, but she did not know if she could ever forgive me. Before she told Diamond she was ready to leave, she looked at me and told me that I am probably everything that Michael had ever hoped for and that that may not necessarily be a good thing for me.

When I crawled into bed that night, I could not help but to think about what Diane had said. I was not sure if she said it to leave doubt in my mind about my relationship or if she was saying something she honestly thought to be true. I know that Michael has demons; I've seen and experienced them firsthand. I also knew that tackling this new life with him would not be easy, but I would never be able to let him go. As soon as Michael crawled into bed next to me and put his arms around me, it did not matter.

I had given my heart and my body to a man that I could marry.

Made in United States
Orlando, FL
09 February 2024